Choosing Us

More Than Friends #10

Aria Grace

Choosing Us

Published by Surrendered Press

CHAPTER ONE

STEVE

Holding the black garment bag up, I unzip it to peek inside. It's been years since I've put on a monkey suit. I can't even remember the last time. I hate to admit it, but I'll be surprised if it still fits considering I spend a lot less time in the gym than I used to.

Since Joey moved in two years ago, my priorities have shifted. I no longer spend hours on end at the gym, trying to hide from the loneliness that was threatening to suffocate me at one point. Now my time is split between hanging out with him and growing my pastry business.

The expansion from just one waffle cart downtown to a kiosk in the mall has taken up a lot of time. Too much of my time. Time that should have been devoted to my little duck. But now that the kiosk is staffed and the holiday season is basically over, I feel like I can breathe again. And the only thing I want to breathe right now is the sweet scent of Joey's thighs as I nuzzle my head between them.

I tap out a quick text to the man that should be naked and under me.

YOU STILL THERE?

He responds within seconds.

SORRY. LEAVING IN 5. PROMISE.

YOU SAID THAT 20 AGO. WE CAN'T BE LATE.

COMING. The text came through and then a second quickly followed. **ACTUALLY, MAYBE YOU SHOULD BE COMING. GO TAKE THE EDGE OFF. I'LL BE THERE SOON. LOVE YOU.**

I'M SAVING IT FOR YOU. GET HERE!

I drop my phone on the dresser and look at the bag again. I might as well get dressed. No sense in us both rushing around right before we have to leave.

The tux pants still fit like a glove. A bit snugger in the ass than I remember, but that's probably from all the additional flexing I do now. Joey likes me to fuck him standing up, holding his weight on my bent legs. It's the best quad and glute workout I've ever done.

Glancing at my watch, I shake my head. It's been twenty minutes and Joey still isn't home. I pick up the phone, but instead of texting again, I decide to call.

"Pot of Gold. Joey speaking." His sweet voice still makes my stomach flutter when I hear it.

"Have they commandeered your cell phone too?" Joey devotes all of his time to the LGBT youth center that once took him in off the streets. The organization, affectionately known as The Pot, specializes in helping teens and adults get back on their feet, usually after being cut off by family members or running away from a bad situation.

My little duck found himself at their doorstep one night when he was only twenty-two. He was attending the University of Oregon when his parents fell on hard times. They couldn't cover his tuition payments anymore so when he was asked to vacate the premises during the holiday break, The Pot was his only option. They gave him a place to sleep until he found the job at Paddles that eventually brought us together.

"Steve? What?" I can hear the confusion in his voice as he fumbles with the phone. "Oh, sorry, Ace. I've been answering the house phone all day. What's up?"

"Me." I don't even try to hide my frustration. "And I'm getting tired of waiting."

"Shit, it's already eight!" I hear keys and rustling in the background. "I'm leaving now. I'll be there in ten."

"Be safe, baby," I whisper before the connection ends.

True to his word, Joey runs through the front door ten minutes later and barrels upstairs. From my seat on the couch, I only catch a glimpse of the blond angel as he strips off his jacket and shoes.

"I need a quick shower and then I'll be ready. What time do we have to be there?"

"We have to leave at nine," I call up just before I hear the shower turn on above me.

I flip the page of the franchising book I've been studying. Several people have approached me about licensing the Waffle Haus name or setting up shops across the country, but I haven't gotten far in the process yet.

When our relationship was new, I didn't want to ever leave Joey's side. But now that he's busy with The Pot, I have some time to consider the expansion plans more seriously. Not only does the name Waffle Haus get all the hipsters hard over its European flare, but my new recipe for gluten free corn-based waffles has every allergy-phobic mom within a hundred miles picking up bulk orders for their wheat sensitive kids.

Joey walks down the stairs at eight forty and I immediately stand and stare at his beautiful form. He's the most perfect man I've ever seen. The blue eyes that I can get lost in for hours seem to twinkle as he lifts his arms and twirls around for my inspection. "So, how do I look?"

"Like a fucking angel." My words are spoken on an exhale as I slowly trail my eyes down and back up his body. "Come here."

Joey slowly slinks to me, his eyes never dropping from mine as he stops a foot away. "You look delicious too."

One of my hands moves to the nape of his neck while the other slides beneath his jacket and flattens on his back. "We don't have time for more than a taste."

Joey's eyes drift shut as I pull his body flush to mine and capture his lips with my hungry mouth. I can't stop myself from ravaging his pouty lips and minty fresh tongue. I suck it in my mouth, imagining it's the tip of his dick I'm milking.

I want to drag him back upstairs and into our bed, but we don't have time. I promised Vinnie we'd get to the party early so I could help direct the catering staff. He was a nervous wreck when we talked on Christmas, convinced they wouldn't know when to bring out each appetizer or who to go to if anything went wrong. As the only person with any kind of food service experience, I agreed to take point so he and Chance could enjoy the formal party they planned for New Year's Eve.

I've also been asked to help with the second part of their party, but I promised not to tell Joey what that is. All he knows is I don't want them to be stressed about crab cakes or goat cheese crostinis.

"I need you, Ace." Joey tilts his head back as I lean down to kiss his neck. He's still warm from his shower and I can't resist. There's no way I'll get through the night without taking him right now. "Please."

Gliding both palms down to his ass, I grip firmly and lift Joey off the ground. His legs wrap around my waist as he grinds his growing cock into my belly. Shifting him so I'm carrying his weight in one arm, I wedge my hand under his ass and undo my belt and zipper. Joey's thighs clench around me and he raises even higher to give me better access to the fabric separating us.

Once I get my pants loose and on the floor, I drop onto the sofa with Joey straddling me. His mouth is back on mine, furiously sucking my tongue and moaning into my mouth while he pulls out of his own pants and maneuvers them to his knees. With his feet planted flat on the cushions beside my hips, his hole is perfectly positioned over my weeping cock.

Before I can gather my wits enough to find some lube, Joey smears the few drops of precum that have leaked from my tip across his pucker and pushes down onto me.

"No, baby." I try to stop him, but the dry friction feels so good. So tight. "Wait."

With eyes scrunched closed, he shakes his head and spits onto his hand then rubs the moisture over my shaft. "I like it. I need this."

I keep my gaze glued to his face as he lowers fully onto me. A light sheen of sweat covers his forehead and his breath is shallow for a minute while his body adjusts. It's like he was made to take me. To accept my length and grip me in heat like no other ever has.

"Are you okay, baby?" I brush the blond strands away from his forehead then trail my fingers down his jaw. "We can get lube."

"It's good." He slowly lifts off me then drops back down. "It's perfect."

I know he's hurting, but if this is what he needs, this is what I'll give him. Dropping slow and loving kisses across his face and neck, I guide him up and down my cock, taking as much of his weight in my arms as I can.

Joey's long, pink cock is pointing straight at me, just begging to unload down my throat.

Fuck, I want that too.

But we don't have time. We're already going to be late, so every minute we take is just adding to the stress building up over at The Heathman Hotel where Chance and Vinnie are setting up their gala.

Flexing my hips so I'm angled better, I drop Joey hard, pressing into the ball of nerves that I know so intimately.

"Again." His panted word is so sexy, so devastatingly erotic that I feel my balls draw up. He has a power over me that can make me shoot with just a few appreciative words.

"Fuck, baby. I'm almost there."

"Hard, Steve." He bounces hard in my lap. "I need it hard."

Lifting Joey almost completely off my engorged head, I pull him down on me with more force than I normally would. Instead of the gasp of pain I'm expecting, I'm rewarded with a deep grunt of pleasure. Joey's hands move to shield his exploding dick from making a mess of us both.

My own release sneaks up on me as I watch his hand fill up with his creamy seed. His tight muscles clench even harder around me, milking every last drop of heat from my pulsating cock before I can breathe again.

He's absolutely perfect.

Chapter Two

Joey

The ballroom Vinnie and Chance rented is amazing. I've never been to a party like this before. The few weddings and anniversary parties I went to as a kid were held in dusty backyards or community rec rooms. Nothing with chandeliers and marble floors.

As soon as we walk in, Vinnie grabs Steve and directs him to a group of servers in white jackets. My heart skips a beat when I see Adam in the group of people heading toward the kitchen.

What the hell is he doing here?

Last time I saw Adam, he was working as a rent boy for Topher. Just like me. Well, not exactly like me. I was there for Topher's personal entertainment.

Adam, on the other hand, took clients. He was only with Paddles for a few months, but he made an impression in that time.

Adam had a baby face, so although he was eighteen when he showed up at Paddle's, he looked even younger. Topher did the requisite background and physical checks and Adam was put on the payroll.

I was already gone by the time he quit, but we were close during the time we were there together. Adam was never really comfortable getting paid for sex. Of course, I didn't blame him. I wasn't either. But the male brothel side of Paddles was a well-oiled machine. If you were nice to the gentlemen, they were nice to you. And if Topher liked you, you got the nicest gentlemen of all.

Being Topher's houseboy was okay most of the time. I didn't like when he passed me around to his friends, but it wasn't too bad. Usually. Not unless Topher was high. Toward the end of my six months there, he was high more often than I was okay with.

Lost in my little trip down memory lane, I almost don't notice Steve stepping back to my side with two servers following close behind him.

Adam's teal green eyes lock on mine and a wide smile breaks across his face.

"Joey?" He steps closer and holds the tray of full champagne flutes to the side. "Is that you?"

"Hi, Adam." I nod and step to his side, wrapping him in a half hug while trying to ignore the heat of Steve's glare on the back of my head. "It's great to see you."

Steve's hand lands on my arm and closes possessively around my bicep. "Baby, do you want to introduce me to your friend?"

I nod and pull back without taking my eyes of Adam. He's different. Older, just barely looking legal though he must be twenty-one if he's serving alcohol. But there's something else. Something pained in the way he smiles at me then glances at my body builder boyfriend.

Moving away from Adam, I curl into Steve's side. "Steve, this is Adam. He used to work at Paddles. Adam, this is my boyfriend, Steve."

Adam's eyes grow wide as he takes in my words. "Wow, Joe. You did good."

I lean up and place a soft kiss on Steve's smooth cheek. "Yeah, I did."

"It's good to meet you, Adam." Steve holds out his arm while pulling me in a little tighter.

"You too." Adam's voice is barely above a whisper as he shakes Steve's hand.

I'm watching Steve's face, trying to read his thoughts. He gives nothing away as he stares intensely at Adam.

Adam's head is down as if he's watching his shoes. I wait a moment for him to look up again, but he doesn't. "Hey, are you okay?"

Adam takes a deep breath and forces a smile. "Yeah, I'm great." He holds the tray out in front of us. "Would you like some champagne?"

"Sure." I grab a glass then offer it to Steve. He accepts the flute, but keeps his attention on Adam, appraising him with a steely gaze that used to make me tremble in fear. I still tremble under his stare, but now it's in a good way.

Steve turns to the front door as a group of guests file in. "I'd love to chat more, but people are probably waiting for drinks."

Adam inhales sharply as if he's been slapped. "I'm sorry. I'll do better." He turns and rushes over to greet the newcomers with a glass of bubbly.

"Why the frown?" Steve asks, running a finger along my lower lip.

I force a smile and nod in Adam's direction. "I think something's wrong with him."

Steve's eyebrows furrow. "Why do you say that?"

"I don't know." I shrug, really not knowing what I mean. I can't put my finger on it, but something is different about Adam. He used to be playful and sweet. Now he seems nervous and anxious.

My mind goes to The Pot and a few of our regular guests. Most of the people there are trying to get their life on track, but a few are really messed up. Addicts that can't think past their next fix. Either victims of early abuse or recent circumstances, they all have that hollow gaze and pained expression that I caught a glimpse of in Adam.

"You guys were close?" Steve asks, speaking quietly so we aren't overheard.

I nod instead of trying to form the right words.

Steve taps my jaw with his finger so I'll turn to him. "Words, please. If he's a friend, I want to know about him."

I pull my lower lip between my teeth before looking into Steve's sea green eyes. "Yeah, we were close. He hung out in the penthouse with us when he wasn't with clients."

"So you guys were together?" Steve doesn't have to spell out his meaning. He's asking if we've had sex.

As much as I hate talking about guys before Steve, I promised I'd never lie to him so I square up my shoulders and nod. "Yeah, a few times. He seemed like a lost kid that just needed someone to love him."

"Did you?" Steve's jaw is tight, but he's trying to stay neutral.

"What?" I ask. "Love him?"

Steve's head dips once in a nod.

"I didn't know him well enough to love him." I step into Steve's chest and exhale as his strong arms wrap around me, grounding me with his love. "But I did care for him. And I hope he's okay now."

~**~

As soon as Steve steps away to check on something in the kitchen, Adam is back at my side.

"So what are you doing these days?" he asks, glancing around anxiously.

"I'm living with Steve and volunteer over at Pot of Gold. I spend a lot of time there."

Adam's eyebrow lifts. "Is that the shelter over on Columbia?"

"Yeah." I put a hand on his shoulder. "You know it?"

I swear Adam's cheeks pink up before he quickly shakes his head and turns away. "I'll talk to you later."

Steve is right behind me, rubbing circles on my back. "Well?"

"Well what?" I ask.

"Is he okay?"

I shrug and watch as Adam moves around the room. Thankfully, our friends start to arrive, so we're distracted long enough for me to see Adam walk out the back door with his cell phone in his hand. As soon as he walks back in fifteen minutes later, I pull Steve along to talk to him.

"Adam," I call as he turns to walk in the same direction we're heading. "Hold up."

Adam stops, but doesn't look back. Tugging Steve so he's close at my side, we round on Adam so we're almost blocking him from escape. "Are you really okay? I feel like something's different about you. Did something happen?"

"A lot has happened." Adam doesn't look up from the spot on the ground he's inspecting. "But I'm fine."

I look at Steve for approval to move in closer. After holding my gaze for a moment, he offers a curt nod and slides his hand under my jacket so his thumb is hooked over my belt. The possessive grip he has on me gives me the confidence to help out a friend in need.

"Adam, look at me," I say quietly, resting my hand on his shoulder and giving him a squeeze. He leans into my touch then slowly looks up at me. "Please let us help you. Whatever you need, Steve and I can help."

Adam's eyes go wide as he looks to Steve, probably afraid that my close proximity will earn him an ass-kicking.

Steve offers a genuine smile and Adam huffs out a deep breath. Whether from shock or relief, I'm not sure, but the tension in his body lessens.

"After I left Paddles—"

"Adam, my man, is that you?" Before Adam can say whatever he finally has the nerve to say, Dylan and Spencer approach us. "You look good, kid."

Dylan pulls him into a hug with Spencer watching from just a step behind him.

"Dylan. Hey!" Adam plasters on a fake smile and pats Dylan's back awkwardly before pulling out of his embrace. "How are you?"

"Great." He turns to Spencer and stretches out his arm. Spencer walks straight into Dylan's side with a content look on his face. "This is Spencer, my boyfriend."

Adam turns to Spencer and holds out his hand. "Good to meet you, man."

"You too." Spencer is one of Steve's closest friends and someone I'll always be grateful to. Seeing him and Dylan so happy together always makes me smile.

"So is everyone shacking up these days? I didn't expect to see you settle down before you were like, forty."

"When you find the right person, it just happens."

The smile on Adam's face drops and he takes a step back. "I gotta get back to work." He waves a hand over his white jacket and black slacks. "Enjoy the party."

"Is he okay?" Spencer asks the question that has been bothering me since I first saw Adam. "He seemed anxious to get away from us."

"I hope so."

~**~

The main event of the evening comes at a quarter to twelve. The lights dim and all eyes are on Chance and Vinnie on a raised platform in front of the floor to ceiling windows.

It's obvious what's about to happen even before I see Steve step out from behind a closed door with a leather bound notebook in his hand.

That little sneak didn't tell me they were actually getting married. I suspected it, but didn't think he'd have any insider information. I didn't even know he could be involved in a wedding. Unless, of course, it was his own.

Just the image of Steve and I standing up in front of our family of friends with the happy sounds of love and encouragement all around us makes me grin like a school girl. Steve and I have talked about getting married, but with our busy schedules over the past year, I can't imagine when we'll actually fit it in.

"Do you believe in this kinda thing?" Adam's quiet whisper startles me as he takes a step closer to my ear.

"What kinda thing?"

"Marriage. Weddings." He glances at me then up to Steve. "Love."

"Of course I do." Steve pronounces them officially off the market and the room explodes in a chorus of whistles and shouts as the new husbands kiss for the first time. I swipe a tear off my cheek right as Steve looks over to me and winks. "It's all I've ever wanted."

Adam doesn't respond. When I finally look at him, he's a little green, like he's going to be sick.

"I hope you find it." He turns away, a raincoat now covering up his uniform. "Take care, Joey."

Adam disappears in the crowd as they wait for the countdown to midnight. According to my watch, we're less than thirty seconds away from the new year. I'm torn between following Adam and making sure I'm there for Steve when the clock strikes twelve.

One glance up at Steve's adoring face resolves any hesitation I'm feeling. Without looking away from those sea green eyes, I walk straight into his waiting arms. Steve's mouth closes over mine before people start counting out loud.

By the time the room erupts into cheers and noise makers around us, Steve and I are out of breath.

The start of another amazing year with the man I love.

CHAPTER THREE

ADAM

I couldn't stay in there another second. The weight of all that happiness was suffocating. It hurts so much to witness something I'll never experience.

I've only ever loved one man and only ever felt loved back by that same man. And now he is practically married and living with some big ass daddy. The fantasies I've been holding on to about running into Joey and becoming a part of his life again were officially crushed tonight.

Not having anywhere to go sucks in general, but in moments like this, I just want to crawl into a real bed and cover my head with a pillow. Unfortunately, that's not an option for me. I've screwed up too many times to get that back.

It's after two in the morning and people are still on the streets, but the crowds are thinning. The few buses that are still running will only have a few more stops before they park for the night. It's not worth getting on one when I'll have to get back off in twenty or thirty minutes.

Although I haven't given in to the temptation in months, I find myself buying a pack of razors at the twenty-four hour drug store then heading straight toward Waterfront Park. It's a hike, but I know I'll have privacy until the buses start up again.

The bench I once sat on with Joey while we watched the sunset is deserted like it always is at this time of night. I sit in the center and stare out over the water, wishing things could be different. Wishing I made better choices all those years ago, even though it probably wouldn't have mattered.

Joey left Paddles first. Well, he escaped and took out Topher, our boss slash owner in the process. I don't know the whole story, but one day I was indebted to

Topher for four thousand dollars I owed my dealer, and the next day, Topher was gone and I was free.

I left Paddles as soon as I heard it was safe to go. At the time, I didn't think I'd ever see Joey again. I planned to stop peddling my ass and get a respectable job in an office or something. Do the kind of work I could tell people about when I met someone in a coffee shop.

Instead, I found myself homeless and at the mercy of Lee, the bastard that promised to take care of me but used me as a punching bag for the past year.

I shouldn't have stayed as long as I did, but I can't change things now. At this point, I have to suffer through the consequences. I'm not even sure when I unwrapped the package and pulled out a razor, but my hand instinctively pulls the leg of my jeans up to my knee while the other presses the blade into the fleshy part of my exposed calf.

With my ankle resting on the opposite knee, I can finally relax, focused on nothing but the sharp sting of broken skin. The broken dreams can be addressed some other time. Right now, I can't think about those. No time for 'what if' or 'why me' when a thick stream of blood has formed a line straight down my calf and is dripping onto the concrete below.

After the initial sting starts to wear off, and the weight of what I've just done is settling in, a cloud opens up above the city and fat rain drops explode across my skin. The red stream turns into a pinkish river as new paths are formed and the blood is diluted.

I throw my head back and let the cold water wash away the tears now flowing down either side of my face. This isn't how I pictured my life, but this is the hand I was dealt and this is how I'll have to play the round.

Despite the cold water and brisk winter air, I manage to doze off on the bench. I don't generally let myself sleep at night. It's dangerous to be unprotected and completely vulnerable, but the lure of escape is too tempting. I have to give in to the darkness for just a little while longer.

Eventually, my eyes open to the rising sun over the river. An orange glow lights up the morning as if it's a perfect spring day. I want to appreciate the beauty, but the pounding in my head is too much. I shouldn't have stayed out in the rain all night. Migraines aren't pleasant on a good day, but when you're homeless, they really blow.

I force myself up and head toward the MAX station. It's early, but there should be a train coming soon and I plan to be on it.

The gym is closed for the holiday so I can't hang out there, staying out of the elements like I usually do. That ten dollar a month membership not only allows me to shower every day, but the manager lets me leave my padlock overnight so I can store my work uniform and the few articles of clothing I still own.

Today, my day will be spent hopping on and off public transportation and looking for an open Starbucks to charge my phone. Another shitty start to another shitty year.

Chapter Four

Steve

"Rachel's feeling nauseous, again, and I need to go close up the kiosk."

"Oh, is she okay?" Joey's previously distracted voice is now concerned. He's such a caring man. He adores Rachel like a sister and worries every time the woman sneezes.

"She says it's nothing, but I think she's pregnant." A whole second passes before Joey is squealing in my ear.

"Pregnant? Really? I'm gonna be an uncle again?"

I laugh at his excitement. I didn't realize he'd be so thrilled by the idea of having another baby around.

He's such a mother hen. When Rachel and Sam let us babysit four-year-old Kaylie on their date nights, Joey hovers over her like a little old lady. You would think she's made of glass by the way he keeps his eyes on her.

"She hasn't confirmed anything yet, but Sam has been bugging her about another baby since they got married. And last week, she puked in a waste basket when I was there to sign checks."

"I hope she is. She's such a good mom." Joey's voice sounds wistful. "We need more like her in this world."

"Is everything okay with you, baby?"

"Not really." The pain in his voice is suddenly obvious and I want to kick myself for not recognizing it sooner.

"What's going on?"

"Do you remember that guy, Kurt, I was telling you about? The heroin addict?"

"Yeah." Joey talks about a lot of the people that pass through The Pot, but that guy stands out in my memory. According to Joey, Kurt was paranoid when he was sober, but completely lucid when he was high. "What about him?"

"He's missing. A few of his buddies came by looking for him and now we're starting to get worried."

"I'm sure he'll turn up, little duck. You know how these things go."

"Yeah, I know." Joey isn't convinced, but I hope my words offer at least a small amount of comfort. "Probably."

"I'll be home as soon as l can," I say. "I love you."

"Love you too, Ace."

~**~

"Are you sure there isn't anything you want to tell me?" I ask Rachel as she's washing her hands. "Any *news* that you'd like to share?"

Rachel tilts her head in my direction and raises an eyebrow. "What do you mean?"

I shrug, feigning innocence. "I don't know. Maybe some announcement of a delivery in the coming months. Something that might require Joey to start searching for another giant panda bear to match Kaylie's?"

31

"I love that boy, but I will tear off his fingernails if he brings another giant stuffed animal into my house. That beast collects more dust than my Swiffer."

I bust up laughing. "He said his niece likes Pandas. I wonder what his future niece or nephew will like. Elephants? Hippos? Maybe dinosaurs?"

"God, if it's a boy, I don't—" She stopped herself then glared at me. "Dammit, Steve. I wasn't going to say anything for another month. You can't tell anyone."

A wide grin spreads across my face. "Joey and I will keep it quiet. We promise."

She shakes her head, knowing there is no way Joey will be able to keep something like this to himself. If he isn't vining his congrats by breakfast, I'll be surprised.

Rachel's finger lands in the middle of my chest with a thump. "If my mother finds out about this before we see her on her birthday, heads will roll."

I have to laugh as I raise my hands in surrender. "Okay, okay. I'll make sure he knows you're serious about this secret thing. When's her birthday?"

"Next Saturday, on the twentieth."

"I'll declare a social media free zone on the topic until the twenty-first."

"Can't you just keep your pie hole shut for another week? Then I'll tell him myself."

I give her a guilty smirk.

"What?" Rachel knows me too well.

"I already told him I thought you might be preggers."

"You knew?" Her hands fly to her belly to smooth down her shirt. "Am I showing? Can you already tell?"

"No, no." I wrap an arm around her shoulder. "You look great. I just figured with all the recent puking, it might be morning sickness."

She barks out a laugh. "More like twenty-four-hours-a-day sickness. I can't keep anything down."

"It'll pass soon. Then we won't be able to stop you from eating everything in sight!" I wiggle my eyebrows so she knows I'm teasing.

She narrows her eyes for a moment then leans forward and plants a kiss on my cheek. "Thanks for closing up. I wouldn't have made it through the night."

"Go home and tell Sam we're happy for you guys. If you need us to watch Kaylie, just holler. You know Joey loves picking her up from school."

"Yeah!" She huffs. "Then he takes her out for ice cream and brings her home all sugared up."

"He tells me that's what nice uncles do. Apparently I'm the mean uncle because I never want ice cream."

"You're not the mean one because of the ice cream." Rachel laughs. "You're mean because you don't let her paint your nails."

"Speaking of, you need to teach that girl how to stay in the lines. Joey's toes were all jacked up last weekend."

She shakes her head as she lifts the hinged counter to step out. "There's a reason why I don't let her touch my nails."

"And that is?" I ask, waiting for her profound words of maternal wisdom.

"She's four, Steve. Four-year-olds don't paint in the lines."

"I'll let Joey in on that little secret."

"Night!"

"Night, Rach." I glance at my watch as a customer walks up to the counter. Nine o'clock can't come soon enough.

CHAPTER FIVE

JOEY

The energy at The Pot has been weird all day. People seem antsy. Anxious. I don't know if it's the non-stop rain, but something just feels wrong.

"I'm heading out with Bryce to look for Kurt." Kim is pulling her jacket off the coat rack by the door. "You gonna stay much longer?"

I pull the chewed up pencil out of my mouth and look at her. "Um, no. I'll probably head out soon too."

"Okay, just be careful driving home. It's practically a typhoon out there."

I shiver just thinking about being stuck outside. "Where are you guys looking?"

"We're going to drive through Kelly Butte Natural Preserve to see if anyone has seen him out there. Then we'll swing by Waterfront. He stays at both places so hopefully we'll find him."

"What are you going to do if you find him?" On particularly wet nights, The Pot fills up quickly. We try not to ever turn anyone away, but once the beds are full and the floors are all littered with bodies in sleeping bags, it's hard to justify going to find someone just to bring them back.

"We just want to make sure he's fine. He's usually here every few days, so people are getting worried. There's been some bad black going around. I'll feel better if I know he's alive."

I nod then blurt out my next words without thinking. "I'll go to Waterfront. It's on my way home anyway. Call me if you find him before I do."

"Will do. Have a good night, Joey."

"Yeah." I shut down the computer I was using to pay some bills then stand to leave as well. "You too."

~**~

Looking for someone on a dark and stormy night is even harder than it sounds. I can't see my hand in

38

front of my face without my flashlight blazing. And because I don't want anyone to think I'm a cop, I keep the light mostly shielded. Only a dim beam illuminates the pathway in front of me.

There are a few corners where junkies are known to party, so that's where I start. Under a thick copse of trees, four people huddle together under a tarp. Keeping my voice friendly and my light low, I call out toward the group, "Is Kurt with you?"

No response so I take a few steps closer. One guy jumps up while the others fumble around behind him.

"Who the hell are you?"

"Hey, it's cool, man. I'm not a cop." I turn the light toward myself so they can see my plain clothes. "Just looking for a friend. Do you know a guy named Kurt?"

A girl turns on a headlight, almost blinding me with the beam before she clicks it into red mode. "I know Kurt. What do you need from him?"

"I don't need anything." I slowly turn the light toward her face so I can see her without shining it directly in her eyes. "Just checking to see if he's okay. I've been trying to reach him for a few days."

She shakes her head then looks at the half-conscious guys next to her. "Nah, it's been a while, but he was fine the last time I saw him."

That's helpful. *Not.*

"Well, if you see him, can you tell him to go see Joey?"

She nods and leans back against the tree.

I hate to leave them there, but The Pot is almost at capacity. I should just turn away and keep looking for Kurt, but I can't do that. "Hey, if you guys need a place to stay, The Pot of Gold on Columbia can give you a dry place to sleep."

The girl laughs. "Thanks, man, but we're good here."

They're definitely not good, but I learned a long time ago that trying to help someone that isn't looking for help is a waste of everyone's time.

"Okay, well, take care of yourselves."

No one even looks up as I turn and head out. There's a person on a bench near the water so I walk quickly toward them. A street light casts just enough light over the person that I can tell it's a man, about the size of Kurt.

Taking longer strides, I hope it's Kurt and he's willing to go to The Pot tonight. He's a good guy that has made some bad choices in life. His mom was a junkie and that's all he's ever known. She overdosed when he was fourteen and he started using right after that. He once joked that he was just carrying on the family tradition. Nothing had ever seemed less funny than the way he genuinely believed it kept him close to his mother.

"Kurt?" I call out when I'm about ten feet from the man. His feet are up against his ass and his head is tucked into his bent knees. If he didn't startle at my voice, I would have been afraid he was dead.

"What?" The man turns his head and coughs twice into his knees.

The familiar voice makes my blood run cold. Please let this be Kurt.

"Is that you, Kurt?"

"No Kurt here."

The man buries his face into his bent knees again and coughs violently, causing me to take a few steps closer.

"Adam?" I whisper as I raise my light across his curled up body. "Is that you?"

Adam's legs hit the ground and he stands at attention like a solider at boot camp. "Joey? Hey, how's it going?"

He's trying to sound casual, but it's clearly an act. He's nervous and jittery.

"What are you doing here, Adam?" I look around to see if he's with anyone, but he's totally alone. "It's freezing."

"I'm fine." He runs his palm across his face, wiping off the water collecting there. "I like the peace of being alone out here."

"Can I give you a ride home?" I don't know where he's living, but he shouldn't be walking anywhere in this weather.

"Oh, no." He clears his throat and puts his hands in his pockets. "I'm cool, but thanks."

I move the beam of light directly over his face until he has to squint to keep from being blinded. "No, you're not cool. You need to get out of this rain. That cough sounds bad. Where do you live?"

Adam's head drops and his chin lands on the center of his collar bone. "I'm fine, Joey. Really."

His words are whispered, but the anguish in his voice is unmistakable. I step right up to him and wrap my arms around his shoulders. "What's going on, Adam? Why are you out here?"

Adam's shoulders rise and fall until I feel his arms slowly close around my waist. He completely ignores my question while breathing into my neck. "It's so good to see you."

My hold on him tightens. "Why don't you come back to my place so we can talk?"

His head bobs up and down, but Adam doesn't say a word. After another moment, I release one arm from around his shoulders then start walking back to my car with him pressed tightly to my side.

Chapter Six

Steve

Rain is falling in sheets as I drive the short distance home. I closed up at eight forty because the mall was dead. I normally would have waited it out, but I was anxious to get home to my little duck.

Relief fills me when I see Joey's white Ford Escape tucked away for the night in the garage. I park next to him and practically jog inside, anxious to get out of my damp clothes from the walk through the mall parking lot.

"Baby, I'm home," I call out as soon as I step into the kitchen.

"We're in the family room."

I pause for just a second. Did he say we?

I inhale deeply then walk into the family room. Joey is sitting in the center of the sofa, his body turned toward the guy beside him.

My stomach churns as I take in the scene. This guy doesn't look familiar, but I trust Joey implicitly. I know whatever reason he has for inviting a stranger into our home, particularly when I'm not around, must be a good one.

I round the sofa and stand on the other side of the coffee table, facing Joey and hopefully the guy he was looking for. But it's not Kurt. It's Adam. The guy from the wedding.

Joey's arm lifts for me and my body instinctively moves to him. I drop onto the couch at his back, pulling him almost into my lap. With his weight pressing down on me, I can finally breathe. My head clears as I look into Adam's terrified face for the first time in weeks.

"Hey, baby." I nuzzle into Joey's neck, taking a deep breath of his sweet scent. "What's going on?"

"Adam needs a place to stay for a little while." Joey's hands wrap around mine and squeeze. "I told him he could stay here."

I freeze behind him for two beats then kiss his neck. "Of course."

"It's okay, Joey. I just remembered a friend that said I was always welcome." Adam turns his head and coughs into his shoulder. "I'll be fine."

Adam's voice trembles through his lie then he stands up, as if he's going to leave. He tries to pass us so he can get to the door, but I don't let him. With one hand on his chest, I stop his movement and nudge him back onto the sofa. "It's fine, Adam. We'd be happy to have you as our guest."

"Are you…" Adam looks like he's about to cry. When his tentative gaze moves from my hand on his chest up to my face, I notice his lip is quivering. "Are you sure? I don't want to mess up anything for you guys."

"We're sure, Adam." Joey lifts one hand from mine and reaches out to take Adam's. "We want to help."

I take this as my opportunity to find out what I've just walked into.

"So," I clear my throat and shift my weight so Joey is resting more comfortably against my chest, "what is it that we're helping with?"

Adam's eyes are firmly locked on the unlit fireplace. He doesn't say a word, so Joey speaks up on his behalf.

"I went looking for Kurt at Waterfront and found Adam there. He's between places right now." Joey shakes Adam's hand to get his attention. "It's okay for me to tell him everything, right?"

Adam nods but doesn't look at me. I can tell he's uncomfortable around me, but I don't know why. I may not have been completely warm and friendly when I met him at the wedding, but I don't think I was an asshole. Then again, I've often been an asshole when I didn't realize it.

"He's only working part time for the catering company now that the holidays are over so he hasn't been able to save up money for first month, last month and the deposit on an apartment."

"I do have some money saved so I should be able to get a place soon." Adam's voice is barely a whisper.

"Where were you living before?" I ask.

Adam's body curls forward and his finger pokes through a hole in his jeans. His sharp intake of breath makes Joey and I both look up at his face.

He's gritting his teeth and screwing his eyes shut, as if trying to escape the moment.

Joey leans forward, placing his hand on Adam's neck. "Adam, honey, are you okay?"

Adam startles at the endearment and pulls away. His eyes reflect pure terror as they lock on mine.

"I'm sorry. I should go."

"No." I hold his gaze, refusing to let him move without telling us what the hell is wrong. "You'll stay where you are and you'll tell us everything."

A tear falls down his cheek, quickly followed by another one. Joey scoots closer to Adam and pulls him into a side hug.

"Adam, it's okay. Steve isn't mad at you." Joey gives me a stern look and raises his eyebrows in Adam's direction. "Right, Ace?"

I take in a deep breath then blow it out. Knowing this is what Joey wants me to do, I get up and move to the coffee table in front of Adam. My knees box his in without actually touching him.

"I'm not mad at you, Adam. I promise."

Adam doesn't respond as he pulls away from Joey so his torso is facing me. With his head down, his tears drip straight onto his jeans, leaving little dark spots where they land.

My hand covers Joey's at Adam's nape. "Adam, look at me."

His head shoots up at the command and his eyes lock on mine as he awaits my next order. "Please tell me where you were living before."

"With Lee. Uh, Lee Reynolds let me stay with him until about a month ago."

"Was Lee your boyfriend?"

Adam shakes his head, but doesn't speak. His gaze stays glued to mine so I press on. "Your pimp?"

Adam shutters. "No, nothing like that." He looks over at Joey. "No offense."

Joey lets out a surprised chuckle. "None taken. Steve isn't my pimp."

A horrified expression passes over Adam's face. Again.

"No, I didn't mean that." His whole body is shaking now. "I just mean…well, you know… at Paddles."

"It's okay, Adam." Joey's soothing voice instantly calms the young man in front of me. "You're safe here. No one is mad and no one will hurt you. But we'd really like to know what happened with Lee."

Adam exhales a slow breath then meets my gaze again. "He was my instructor at culinary school. After a few months, we became, I don't know, fuck buddies, I guess."

"Culinary school?" Joey's grin is a welcome addition to this tense conversation. "You went to culinary school?"

"For the past year." Adam nods his head proudly at Joey's excitement.

"That's awesome!"

"So why did you move out?" I ask, getting the conversation back on track. The last time I took a homeless kid in off the street, I had to go toe to toe with a mob boss. I have no regrets and would do it again in a heartbeat, but same as back then, I need to have all the information before I know what to do next. "Where is Lee now?"

The shy smile drops from Adam's attractive face as he turns back to me. "He has a bad temper. After a pretty bad fight we had on Christmas day, I tried to fight back and he kicked me out."

"Out of culinary school?" I ask. "Or out of his house?"

"Both." Adam's eyes hold more shame than sadness.

I rest my hand on his knee then reach out to take Joey's hand. "Well, you're welcome to stay here for as long as you want."

"Thank you, sir." Adam quickly glances at me before dropping his eyes to my hand on his knee. "I won't disappoint you."

I'm not sure what that means, but I don't think he can handle much more tonight. The poor kid looks like he hasn't had a good night's sleep in weeks.

"You can't disappoint me, Adam."

Instead of the smile I'm expecting, Adam flinches and looks devastated. "Oh, of course. I'm sorry."

I frown as I try to decipher what he could possibly mean. Joey just shrugs and leans against Adam's side.

"Why are you sorry, Adam?" I use a tone that allows no option for disobedience.

"For being presumptuous, sir."

I'm starting to understand what he needs and why he's so nervous around me. His submissive nature needs to be commanded. Approved of. That's something I can work with. Joey was in a similar place when he first came into my life. He just needed to know he was safe and cared for.

"Presumptuous about what?" I ask in a calm but firm voice.

"Disappointing you," he whispers.

One glance at Joey and I know he gets where Adam is coming from. He must be seeing all the same traits in Adam that he carried just a few years ago.

"Adam." Joey plays good cop well. His years of experience working with scared and abused youth has taught him how to coax out information without further frightening the person. "Why do you think you were presumptuous about Steve being disappointed in you?"

He shrugs but my hand on his knee flexes enough to remind him I'm expecting an answer.

"He could only be disappointed in me if he cared."

Well, fuck.

"Honey, we do care. Steve and I both care about you." Joey gives me a pointed look, raising one eyebrow in Adam's direction.

"He's right, Adam." I let my knees close around his so he's completely caged in by Joey and I. "We both want you to be here and we both care about you. As long as you keep yourself healthy and strong, you won't disappoint us. Can you promise to do that?"

Adam's chin quivers as he meets my gaze. "I promise to try."

Joey rests his head on Adam's shoulder and pats his back. "That's all we ask for."

I smile and pat the outside of his thigh. "Okay, then it's probably time for us to hit the sack."

Joey will show you to the guest room and we'll be right upstairs if you need us. I wait for Adam to acknowledge me before standing up and ruffling the top of his damp hair with my hand.

"Get some sleep, boy."

CHAPTER SEVEN

ADAM

I still can't believe I'm here. Warm and comfortable in an actual house. Not just a house, a home. It's crazy to think that Joey plucked me off that park bench just a few hours ago. At first, I assumed I was dead and he was an angel sent to collect my soul. Of course, if I thought long enough about it, I would have realized that was absurd. When I die, I won't be going with any angels. Anyone coming for me will be dressed in black and have flames shooting out of his ass.

During the whole ride to his house, I fingered the pack of blades in my pocket. I have one clean razor left that I've been saving. I don't want to use it but I like knowing it's there if I need it.

Lying in the soft bed and listening to muffled conversations traveling through the heating vents, I'm tempted to pull it out of the protective case. Maybe then I can think clearly. I'm so confused by everything that has happened in the past few hours. I just need a few minutes of clarity to figure out what to do next.

As I sit up to go grab the blade, a soft tap on my door startles me.

"Come in," I say, wondering if I'm just hearing things.

The door slowly opens and a beam of light appears at the front of the dark room. "I brought you a bottle of water." Joey is wearing a pair of sweats that hug his compact muscles and nothing else.

He had a great body two and half years ago but he's filled out since then. His previously slender body has turned into that of a sculpted man.

"Thanks."

"Just holler if you need anything. Or go upstairs. We'll leave the door open so don't be afraid to find us."

"Okay," I whisper.

"Adam?" Joey's soft voice causes a wave of tingles to shoot up my spine. "I'm really glad you're here."

As soon as I hear him walk up the stairs, I lean back and close my eyes. I'll figure out what to do tomorrow. Right now, I need to sleep.

~**~

There are footsteps overhead and clanking metal sounds coming from down below. I don't want to wake up, but after a few minutes of enjoying the comfort and warmth of the bed, I finally peel my eyes open. Bad idea. I bury my head in the pillow again.

I feel like shit. I've gotten used to ignoring the constant pain of always being wet and cold. But after one night in a warm, dry bed, my body seems to think it's on vacation.

I've only been out of fight or flight mode for ten hours and my immunity has already given up. My head feels like it's stuffed with cotton and my throat is burning. I turn to sit up but the ache in my body stops me from moving. It's not the good kind of focused ache that I can concentrate on but an overall miserable feeling that makes me want to stay in bed forever.

I cough twice, holding my head at both temples to stop it from shaking. The pounding is like a jackhammer digging out my brain. Every movement I make gouges out another path of pain.

I want to get up and take a shower but I can't find the will to move. My arm flails out until my hand closes around the water bottle. I pull it toward me but a large hand wraps around my wrist and stops the movement.

My eyes fly open and I sit up, ignoring the pain shooting from every bone and muscle in my body. Steve is standing over me with a towel around his neck, sweat dripping down his wide, muscular chest.

The man is pure sex on a stick.

"Sit up and I'll help you."

Unable to disobey my host, I sit up and watch as he unscrews the cap and hands me the bottle of water. I take it but don't drink. Instead, I just stare at Steve's taut, glistening skin. "Thanks."

"Take a drink, Adam."

As if to prove his demand is valid, my chest explodes in a fit of gasping coughs that almost make me vomit from the violence of it.

"Shit, Adam." Steve's hand covers my forehead then curves around the side of my cheek. "You're burning up."

I shake my head and take a sip of the water, attempting to get the coughing under control. "Just a cold. I'll be fine."

"Probably." Steve's hand stays on my cheek for a moment before he moves it back to his hip. "But we're taking you to the doctor. Do you want to take a shower first?"

"Thanks, but I'm okay. I just need to rest. My body is probably in shock from being in a warm bed."

Steve's lips purse and his nostrils flare. "Take a warm shower and Joey will bring you some clean clothes to wear. We'll leave in half an hour."

"Yes, sir." His obvious concern for my well-being, or maybe for his well-being since I'm contaminating his home, warms my heart. "But..."

"But, what?" Steve's green eyes bore holes into mine like he's scrutinizing my every emotion.

"Um, well, I don't have insurance. Can we just go to the clinic downtown? I can pay cash there."

"I'll take care of the visit. Just get ready to go." Steve pats my knee twice then walks out of the room.

~**~

"Mr. Adam Knox?" a nurse in blue scrubs holds open the door. I stand up then Steve and Joey stand up beside me.

I turn to them with a confused expression. "You don't have to go in. I'm okay." I have to turn my head to cough into my bent elbow so I'm not coughing directly into either of those gorgeous faces.

"Adam." Steve's voice is low and deep, vibrating right through my belly to my cock. "I'd like to go in to hear what the doctor says. But if you don't feel comfortable with me being in there, please let Joey go with you."

He wants to go in with me? They both do? Why, so they can check on me?

"I won't lie to the doctor." I look up into Steve's eyes. He's three or four inches taller than me but I square my shoulders and speak with sincerity. "I'll tell him everything."

Steve smiles warmly, placing a hand at the small of my back as Joey takes a step in closer to us. "I know you won't lie, Adam. We just want to know how to take care of you. Is that okay?"

I don't want either of them to go in with me, but I can't find the will to say no. I nod and turn toward the nurse who is patiently waiting with the door held open.

"Right this way, Mr. Knox."

I follow the woman, feeling the presence of Steve and Joey right behind me.

"Please head into exam room two." She points to the first open door on the right. "I left two gowns if you'd like to wear the bottom one open in the back and the top one open in the front. As soon as you're undressed, please use the restroom down the hall to leave a urine specimen then wait for the doctor in the room."

"Thank you." I walk into the small exam room and lift the two cloth gowns from the paper-covered table.

"We can step into the hall if you'd like privacy to change," Steve says as soon as the door is closed behind him.

I shake my head. "That's okay. Just, um." I take a deep breath and turn my back to the men watching my every move. "Well, I have some scars."

"It's okay, honey." Joey's just as accepting as he always was. That much about him hasn't changed. He saw some of my scarring from high school but there are more now. Fresh cuts that he might not be expecting.

I take off the borrowed jacket and pull the sweater over my head without looking over my shoulder once. I slip my arms through the first gown then turn toward Joey and Steve. I feel like I'm wearing a Snuggie blanket. The guys are huddled together in the corner, pretending to read a poster about the stages of fetus development.

With the gown covering the front of my body to mid-thigh, I slip off my jeans. While my backside is exposed to the wall, I slip on the other gown like a jacket so it's hanging open in the front. Everything is covered, including the jagged scars I've carved across my belly and inside my thighs.

The newer lines on my calves are visible but I can't do anything to hide those.

"Uh, I'll be right back."

Steve and Joey both jerk toward me, seeming surprised by my ability to speak.

I leave the room with the plastic jar in my hand and hurry to the restroom. By the time I return, Joey is sitting in the corner chair with my clothes neatly folded in his lap. Steve is standing beside him with his hand behind Joey's neck.

I offer a tight smile as I slide the warm jar of piss over the counter and climb onto the exam table. Just as my lungs explode into a coughing fit, the door opens and an older female doctor walks in with a nurse beside her.

The nurse wraps a blood pressure cuff around my arm and starts jotting down numbers as the doctor washes her hands. When she finally turns around, her eyes widen as she realizes Steve and Joey are both in the room with me.

I open my mouth to explain their presence but I can't. I have no idea why they want to be here so I just stay silent and let the unasked question hang in the air.

The doctor ignores my entourage and clasps her hands in front of her belly. "Good morning, Adam.

I'm Dr. Cheney. What brings you out in this weather?"

I shrug then remember I've got an audience. A cranky audience. "Um, I've got this cold. Well, a cough, I guess."

"Okay." She pulls the stethoscope off her neck and holds it up. "How long have you had the cough?"

"A few days. Maybe a week."

The doctor pulls the outer gown off, exposing my back, then places the cold metal disk onto my skin. I can feel both sets of curious eyes behind me, watching her every move. "What do you do for a living?"

I tense at the question, ashamed to answer in front of Steve and Joey but grateful to not be facing them. "I'm working as a part-time server for a catering company but things have been slow recently."

"I see." She moves the stethoscope to my chest and asks me to inhale and exhale deeply. The inhale is okay but the exhale is more of a barky cough. "I've seen a few cases of walking pneumonia this month. We'll need to do a blood test to confirm, but that's what I'm thinking."

"Is that bad?" I ask, not liking how close the name is to *Walking Dead*.

"It's not great," she says, stepping back to the front of the table. "But, it's treatable. I can give you a course of antibiotics or you can try rest and fluids for a few days. I generally leave it up to the patient for mild cases."

"Rest and fluids are fine with me." And my pathetic checking account. I can't afford to waste a few hundred bucks on meds that aren't one hundred percent necessary.

"Maybe we should take a script for the antibiotics in case you change your mind." Steve's firm but friendly voice almost makes me jump.

Dr. Cheney notices my reaction and narrows her gaze on Steve. "And you are?"

"Adam's roommates. We'll make sure he gets lots of rest and chicken soup. But if that's not enough, I'd feel better knowing he can pick up a prescription." Steve uses the same gentle tone to charm the doctor that he naturally uses when talking to Joey.

She doesn't fall for it.

"And how do you feel about that, Adam?" The doctor returns her focus to me, waiting for my response.

I nod. "Yeah, that's a good idea."

"Okay, then let's get the rest of your physical out of the way before I send you to the lab next door." She pats the back of the table for me to lie down.

"Oh." I look over my shoulder at Joey then back to the doctor. "I don't need a full physical. Just the blood test is fine."

The doctor's eyebrows furrow and she reaches for her clipboard. "Says we're to do a full work up. When was the last time you had a physical?"

I shake my head and let my chin drop to my chest. Fighting it is futile. Obviously Steve asked for the full check-up, probably wanting to make sure I don't have any STDs I might corrode his house with.

I'll sit through the physical but as soon as she sees the scars, I'll never be able to look at Joey or Steve again. With my eyes tightly closed, I lay back on the table and allow her to poke and prod me.

Her hands wrap around my right foot and then my left. She asks me to flex then push against her palm as if testing my strength. When she steps to the side and sees the pink scar on my calf, her fingers immediately probe at it.

"Is this fresh?" she asks quietly.

I nod without speaking.

Steve clears his throat behind me and I know what that means.

"Yes, ma'am."

"When did you cut yourself?" Her question is innocuous enough that it could mean anything. People accidentally cut themselves all the time.

"Um, a few weeks ago." She leans forward to look at it then pulls the gown up higher on my thigh, revealing the rows of old scars, and a few new, that I've hidden there.

"Can you be more specific?" She wants a date. The one thing I don't want to give her. But, I can't think of a better lie so I settle for the truth.

"Um, I think it was New Year's."

Joey's sharp intake of breath makes my eyes sting. Fuck! I don't want him to think it was about him. It was, but he doesn't need to know that. It certainly wasn't his fault.

Like everything else, it was my fault. My fucked up way of dealing with a situation I couldn't control.

"Are you still cutting?" Dr. Cheney finds two rows of newer scabs behind my knees and waits for me to try to lie to her.

I'm certainly tempted.

"Not for a few days." The tear that escapes the watery pools in my eyes is like a metaphor for my life. Never playing nicely with the team. Never staying with the group. Always falling down.

Alone.

"I didn't know anything about this." Steve's sad voice makes me want to kill myself. I've already disappointed him. He's going to hate me now.

"Adam?" The doctor calls me to her attention so I force my eyes open and look at her. "Do you know how dangerous it is to intentionally cut yourself? Not only are you at increased risk of infection but your body can't fight off things like walking pneumonia when it's constantly trying to grow new skin and replace lost blood. Not to mention the fact that HIV is still a very real issue in this country. Dirty needles and knives are everywhere, young man. The risk you're taking can't possibly be worth the moments of escape you're seeking..."

She stops her rant just long enough to take a breath and jot down some notes on her clipboard. "I'd like you to see a therapist about the reasons you have for cutting."

I don't respond, just waiting for the exam to be over so I can head to the gym and change into my own clothes. Maybe I'll even be able to catch a nap before the afternoon rush hour begins because I still feel like shit.

"Adam?"

I nod and smile, pretending to be listening to everything she's saying. I'll agree to go to Mars if it'll get me out of this place any sooner.

CHAPTER EIGHT

JOEY

New Years. That's when Adam started cutting again. I want to jump up and shake him, ask him why he would harm one inch of his perfect skin, but I can't confront him here. Maybe not at all. All I can do is press my forehead into Steve's hip and let him hold me against him. Reminding me that I'm loved and cared for in a way that Adam might not have ever experienced on his own.

By the time we leave the lab where Adam had his blood drawn, we're all tense and anxious. I can sense Steve's dark mood by the way he's walking a few paces ahead of us. He doesn't distance himself very often, but when there's a problem he doesn't know how to fix, he needs space to think about it.

I'm the opposite, of course. When I see a problem, I want to run at it with five different solutions and try them all until something sticks. In this situation, I'm not sure what to do so I just walk close by Adam's side, letting him know I'm here for him without judgment. Steve and I will both help him get past whatever he's going through.

When we get to Steve's truck, I open the front passenger door and duck inside before realizing the door behind me hasn't opened. Adam is standing awkwardly next to the truck.

"Look, Joey." He takes a step forward and bends down in the open door to face me and Steve. "I really appreciate the offer to stay with you but I don't want to get you guys sick. Maybe I'll check out that Pot of Gold place you mentioned and see if they have room, but I can't go back to your place right now."

My hand instinctively reaches for him before he pulls away. "Please, Adam. You need to rest. You can't be wandering around the streets right now. You'll just get worse." I beg him with my eyes to agree. "Besides, you'll be infecting a lot more people if you're out in public than just me and Steve. Please don't leave."

I can sense Steve getting out of the truck, but it's not until his wide body forms a shadow over Adam that I know he's going to handle this.

Steve's palms close over Adam's shoulders and he gently pulls him into a standing position. Adam is breathing in quick pants as Steve holds him against his body. With Steve's steel arm across his chest, Adam isn't going anywhere. Not yet. Hopefully, not ever. After a moment of just standing there, their breaths sync up in a normal rhythm.

"I'm proud of you for being honest with the doctor, sweetheart." Steve's voice is soft against Adam's ear.

A dry sob escapes his throat as Adam's chin dips forward.

"I know you're scared, and maybe even embarrassed, but you have no reason to be. Joey and I care about you and want you to come home with us."

Adam shakes his head even as the tears begin to stream down both cheeks. "I'll be too much of a burden right now. I don't want to cost you any more time or money."

I can't sit by and watch any longer. I get out of the truck, pressing myself against Adam in an emotional group hug.

With the side of my cheek at Adam's ear, I lean forward and place a soft kiss on Steve's lips. "Thank you."

His free hand cradles the back of my neck as he holds me in place, before leaving an equally chaste kiss on the back of Adam's head.

"Can we go home now?"

I nod and pull back, looking into Adam's eyes for agreement. His teeth close over his lower lip but he doesn't disagree.

"Home it is," I say, opening the back door to the truck and waiting for Adam to climb inside.

We swing by Mama Cecily's for a large container of minestrone and a bag of her famous rolls. She isn't open for another hour but when she saw us through the window, she didn't hesitate to let us in. Steve and I can live off that stuff and it's been a while since we've had time to pick it up.

"Soup, then bed," Steve says to Adam as soon as we walk through the front door.

"Yes, sir." Adam's voice is almost inaudible.

I can't tell if he's tired, upset, or both, but he walks straight to the dining table and has a seat, allowing us to serve him a bowl of piping hot soup.

We eat our soup and rolls without a lot of conversation. Steve and I both made arrangements to stay home today so we have all day to play nurse.

I smirk and shift subtly in my seat. Playing nurse actually sounds pretty good right now.

After we're all done eating, I give Steve a questioning look. He tilts his chin down in a nod that only I would recognize.

"Adam, are you ready to go lie down?" I ask softly, as if I need to handle him with kid gloves.

He slides the chair back and stands. Without saying a word, Adam picks up his dishes and walks into the kitchen. I follow him so we can quickly clean up and get him into bed.

Once he's passed out, I find Steve down in the basement, half-heartedly curling a dumbbell.

I slide onto the bench he's straddling and scoot close enough that my thighs overlap his. "So, tell me what you're thinking."

Steve puts down the dumbbell and wraps his hands around my ass, pulling me closer to him.

"He reminds me of you."

"I know." I smile and nuzzle into Steve's neck. His body is hot and sticky from his workout. I can't resist swiping my tongue across his salty skin. "But are you okay with him being here?"

"If you want Adam here, he'll stay here." Steve's fingers knead my ass, making my head roll back as I enjoy the firm but sensual touch.

"It's not weird, right?" I hold my stare until Steve's eyes lock on mine. I want him to be present for this conversation. "I don't want you to be uncomfortable just because Adam and I have a history."

Steve leans forward and snags my lower lip with his teeth, pulling back just enough to shoot an electric bolt into my dick.

"I trust you and love you." Steve's lips graze my chin and rest at my earlobe. "If you want him here for now, forever, whatever. It's okay, baby. I remember what you needed when you were in his situation, and you know better than anyone what he's going through now."

"Which is why I think we're the best people to help him." My elbows lock with my hands clasped behind Steve's head. He's not going anywhere until we talk.

"Is that the only reason you want him to stay?" Steve asks without any hint of emotion on his face. "So we can help him?"

I pull back, checking to see if I've misheard the crack in Steve's voice. "What do you mean? You just said it was okay. That you want him here too."

"I do, baby." The loving way he holds me makes me want to tear his clothes off and worship every inch of his body and soul. But we need this talk. "But I need to know you're completely honest with me and with yourself about your feelings for Adam."

"Steve." My eyes well up and a lump forms in my throat. "What are you saying? You know I love you more than anything in this world. I'd never do anything to jeopardize what we have. If you don't want him to stay here, we can take him to The Pot. Or, I can ask Dylan if he can stay at Paddles for a while. He'll be okay—"

Steve cuts off my rambling with a kiss. Soft at first but within seconds it goes all toe curling, cock lengthening hot. Fuck, this man can kiss.

His arms close around me, caging me against his body as I hop up onto his lap. My balls are resting against his but the denim I'm wearing doesn't give me any of the relief I need despite being cock to cock.

"Wait." I pant out shallow breaths, trying to inhale enough oxygen to speak. "We need to talk."

"We need to come."

"Steve." I let his mouth close over mine for a few seconds as his hand releases the button and zipper of my jeans. "We're not done with this conversation."

"Mmm." He moans into my ear as his hand slides under my zipper and cups my sensitive balls. "Come now. Talk after."

Sometimes it's easier to just give in when Steve really wants something. And I just happen to completely agree with his four-word argument.

When I can finally break away for air, I stand up and shuck off my jeans. My t-shirt is next to fly across the basement while Steve rolls back on the short bench and slips his gym shorts off his legs and into the same corner my shirt landed in.

Knowing what he wants, I climb back onto his lap, facing him with my thighs tightly gripping his waist.

Steve's tongue glides across my lower lip then sweeps inside my mouth and over my teeth. He's taking it slow. His hands press our aligned cocks together, and an excited whimper escapes my chest. I love when he strokes us together like this.

"I love you so much, baby," Steve whispers into my mouth as he slowly pulls up and down on our joined dicks.

"Me too, Ace." A shiver races down my spine as he taps my slit with his fingertip. "I'll always love you. Forever."

"I know, little duck." Steve's hand moves faster as he nips along my jaw to my earlobe. "And I'd do anything to keep you happy. Anything you want. Just ask and I'll do it."

"Yes, that." My hip thrusts up into his fist, sliding easily with all the fluid we're leaking. "Just like that."

Steve's mouth covers mine again and I dig my blunt fingernails into his shoulders, riding his hips. Fucking his fist. God, he feels good.

When I can't hold back the orgasm any longer, I erupt between us, showering both of us in ropes of white cream.

"God, baby." Steve's grip on my neck tightens as his mouth crashes against mine. The warm streams that splash onto my belly instantly make me hard again. "You're absolutely perfect."

CHAPTER NINE

ADAM

I know I shouldn't be intruding on their lives in this way but I can't bring myself to leave. I've never been in a house with so much love and respect. It's addictive. Even if the love and respect isn't necessarily directed at me, I still like to be near it, soaking it in by osmosis.

Whatever Joey did to find a guy like Steve to take care of him must have been amazing. Pulling-a-kid-out-of-a-burning-building kind of amazing to have the adoration of such a strong and loving man.

Steve would walk to the ends of the earth for Joey, and while I'm here as his guest, I sometimes feel like he might do the same for me. After five days of rest and fluids and lying in bed, I'm finally feeling better. They've shifted their lives around to take care of me, as if I were family. Not like real families that slap you for spilling your juice or beat you with a belt if you break a glass. The kind of family you see on TV. Where you put your own needs on the backburner to meet the needs of those you love.

Steve does that with Joey. And though it comes as no surprise to me, Joey does it right back to Steve. If one is hungry, the other will get him something to eat. If one is cold, the other will bring him a blanket or start a fire.

With the way they've been taking care of me for the past week, it's easy for me to pretend I'm part of their little family. Not just as a friend or a guest but really part of their family unit.

But I don't let myself get too carried away in that fantasy. The love I feel for Joey will always be there but he's no longer in a position to reciprocate it. He has Steve. And Steve has given him everything he could ever want. There's no room for me long term.

I just need to enjoy this time with them while I can, living vicariously through their relationship until I have to leave. I've already set a mental timer for two months. Now that I have a place to live, I can get a full time job and save enough money to rent a room somewhere. For now, I enjoy the game and pretend I belong here.

"The auditions are the best part!" Joey hands me a bowl of popcorn then drapes himself across the sofa with his head in Steve's lap. "I don't even care about the rest of the show. I just love watching the tryouts."

Steve laughs. "You just love watching people make fools of themselves."

Joey smacks his lover's chest playfully. "No, I don't. I feel bad for the really horrible singers. But let's put the blame where it belongs. What kind of friend lets their tone-deaf friend try out for a singing contest on national TV? It's really sad, actually."

"So, why do you watch it?" I ask, never having watched a single episode of American Idol.

"Because it's amazing." Joey shushes me as he points the remote at the huge TV on the wall. "It's starting. You'll see."

By the time the first commercial comes on, I've rolled my eyes at least six times and cringed twice that often. Steve and I have even shared a few amused glances when Joey got caught up in a song and felt the need to sing along.

When some chubby guy with bad teeth and day glow orange hair begins to belt out *Happy* by Pharrell Williams, we all bust up laughing. That is, until Joey starts shaking his jazz hands and bouncing around on Steve's lap.

Steve leans down and whispers something about how happy Joey is making 'little Steve.' I know I shouldn't be eavesdropping on their private conversation but just the image of Steve getting hard while Joey's head is in his lap has me getting hard too. From where I'm sitting on the love seat, I know they can't see the bulge forming under my sweats but I still shift sideways, tucking one foot under my ass so I'm well hidden.

After a few of those people with shitty friends that have lied to them about having talent are booted off the stage, a carpenter looking guy in torn jeans and a skin tight t-shirt stalks the stage.

All three of us let out an appreciative sigh as he introduces himself. He starts singing *Father Figure* by George Michael, I get butterflies. But when Steve's deep voice joins him, I swoon.

I will be your father figure.

I have had enough of crime.

I will be the one who loves you.

Til the end of time.

I can't take my eyes off the scene beside me. Steve is singing quietly into Joey's ear as Joey smiles adoringly at him through glistening eyes.

Looking back up at Steve, I realize he's staring right at me. His wink and smile are meant to assure me that he's not mad but it doesn't work. Nothing could relieve the knot in my gut that has suddenly formed. I feel that full body ache that has kept me in bed for days. I just want to be alone. I can't watch them anymore.

Steve and Joey are too happy. Too much in love. Too big of a reminder of what I'll never have. Even when I'm with someone, it's not like this. Not a home. A family.

I turn back to the TV before Steve can see my tears falling.

"I'll love you 'til the end of time too, Ace," Joey says softly. I can hear the smack of a kiss but I don't dare look. Not with tear streaks running down my face.

Pretending to press on my temple, I rub the moisture into my skin so they don't know how much I'm affected by their public affection. They don't need to know how envious I am of what they have. Together and individually, they're both perfect men that deserve each other.

The kind of men that I can only dream of being with.

Loving.

Being loved by.

With only five minutes left of the show, I take slow and even breaths. I can get through the final audition and make my way to the guest room without too much of a scene. Joey and Steve are so caught up in each other they've probably forgotten I'm even here.

When a teenaged girl, no more than fifteen or sixteen, walks up in front of the judges, I'm grateful that some pop song from Taylor Swift or Ariana Grande will probably wrap up the show and offer me a blessed escape, giving me the excuse to hide away from the men that have been the center of my every waking and sleeping thought for the past month.

"I'll be singing *Someone Like You* by Adele."

My heart almost stops when she begins the most soulful rendition of that song I've ever heard. I try to focus on the sound and not lyrics but I can't avoid the elephant in the room.

I hate to turn up out of the blue, uninvited

But I couldn't stay away,

I couldn't fight it

I had hoped you'd see my face

And that you'd be reminded that for me,

It isn't over

I can't hold back the quiet sob as I realize how those few words sum up my life. I want Joey back. I want what he has. Fuck, if I'm honest with myself, I want Steve too. I want their family. Their life. Their love.

Standing quickly, I keep my back to them as I walk past Steve and Joey. "Good night," I call over my shoulder, hoping they can't hear the quiver in my voice.

Chapter Ten

Steve

When Adam rushes past us, I know he's upset. It's not until I turn back to the TV and realize what song is being sung that I have an idea why.

Joey tries to sit up but I place my hand on his chest. "Give him some space."

"Why?" Joey looks at me with questions written all over his face. "What's wrong with him?"

I lean forward and place a kiss on my little duck's forehead. "I'm not sure but I think he's still just adjusting to being here. You can talk to him about it tomorrow."

Joey nods and lifts his head for a real kiss. Bending down, I meet him half way, never able to deny him anything.

"I wish you didn't have to work tomorrow." Joey playfully bites my stomach through my shirt. "You're too yummy to be gone on the weekends too."

"I've got an ad posted for another full-time person. As soon as I get someone hired, I'll be home more often." I slide my arms under Joey's shoulders and knees then stand up with him in my arms. "If I have to double the salary for the weekend shift, I will."

"Promise?" Joey's tongue is swirling figure eights on my neck. I'm hard before we even get to the top of the stairs.

"I promise, baby." Laying him gently on the bed, I hover over his body. "I told you before. Whatever you want. Just ask for it. I'll always give you what you need."

"I know." Joey's hands slide under my shirt, pulling it up as he reaches my chest. "And right now, I need you naked and inside of me."

~**~

My eyes pop open just seconds before my alarm goes off at six on Saturday morning. I don't want to get up and leave these boys, but I've got a busy day ahead of me. I ruefully get out of bed and quietly get ready to leave. Before I head downstairs, I bend over to kiss Joey goodbye. Instead of the sleepy smile I usually get, Joey's eyes pop open and he reaches for my hand.

"Hey, why don't you hire Adam?"

I'm not sure if he's awake or asleep so I kiss his temple. "Okay, we'll talk later."

"No, I mean it. He needs a full-time job and he wants to be a chef. He'd probably love to help you out for a while. It's perfect."

"Maybe when he's feeling better." I run my fingers through Joey's baby fine hair. The blond strands are sticking up in all directions, just the way I love. "Go back to sleep, baby."

When I reach the bottom of the landing, I'm surprised to find a fresh pot of coffee waiting for me and Adam scooping eggs onto a tortilla. "I don't know if you like breakfast burritos but I figured you might not have time to eat so you could take this with you."

I look from the tortilla he's folding up into a perfect burrito to the nervous twitch in his jaw. "You made that for me?"

"Yeah." He wraps the whole thing in a piece of aluminum foil he had waiting on the counter. "Is that okay?"

I shake off the surprise and grin at the thoughtful gesture. "Of course it's okay."

Adam's turquoise eyes flash with pride as a shy smile makes an appearance on his innocent face. I know he's far from innocent but his round face and soft features make him seem younger than his twenty-one years. He makes me just want to hold and protect him.

Holding up my arms, I invite Adam in for a hug. I let him decide what he's comfortable with and he doesn't hesitate.

"That was a very thoughtful thing to do for me, Adam."

He shivers in my arms and holds my waist even tighter.

"You've made me very happy." I rest my chin on the side of his tilted head. "You're a good boy."

"Thank you, sir." Adam melts into me and I'm afraid to let him go. I'm not sure what to do next but I know he needs comfort right now. Unfortunately, I have a huge order of gluten free waffles for a local restaurant that will be picked up in three hours. As much as I want to stay, I've got to start baking.

"Adam, sweetie?"

He turns his head and peeks at me from under long, brown lashes. "Yes."

"Would you like to lay down with Joey? I have to go to work but I don't want to leave you alone."

His eyes go wide. "Really? Is that okay?"

I smile and brush my cheek over his. "Yes, that's okay. I know he won't mind."

"Um, but..." Adam's face is buried in my chest as I wait for him to say words that seem to have been lost.

"Adam, please tell me what you're thinking."

"Well, um, won't you be worried or, um, uncomfortable with me in your bed?"

Even with his face turned down, I can see the pink hue of his cheeks. "I trust you and Joey. I know you'll both behave while I'm gone."

"Oh." Adam seems confused but unwilling to let the opportunity pass unseized. "Then, yes, please. I'd like that."

Holding his hand in mine, I tug Adam up the stairs and to the side of my bed. Joey looks like an angel floating in a cloud of downy white blankets. Leaning over, I run my palm over Joey's forehead, brushing away the strands covering his face.

"Baby," I whisper into his ear, kissing the shell softly. "Wake up for a minute."

"Hmm?" Joey's eyes don't open but he turns his head toward me with a smile. "I'm awake."

"Adam wants to lay down with you for a little while. Is that okay?"

He nods and scoots to the middle of the bed. "Um hmm."

"I love you, little duck." I brush a kiss across his lips then turn to Adam. "Thank you again for breakfast, sweetie."

I brush the hair off Adam's forehead then pull back the side of the comforter so he can climb in beside Joey. After dropping a quick kiss on top of his head, I turn away and leave for work.

Just knowing those boys are together in my bed is going to make it impossible to concentrate on anything but what they would look like naked and begging me to take them.

CHAPTER ELEVEN

JOEY

The bright beams of sunlight finally reach my face and I know it's time to wake up. I kick one leg out, looking for a cool spot in the toasty sheets. When I encounter warm skin, my hand reaches out on reflex, eager to find Steve's hard body lying next to me.

The hard body I find is warm but definitely not Steve's. Then I remember the sleepy conversation from early this morning. Steve brought Adam up to lay with me.

With my hand pressed awkwardly to his side, I release a breath and slide my fingers around to his belly, giving him a quick pat.

Adam tenses under my touch, not even moving his chest up or down to breathe.

"Good morning," I whisper then pull my hand off his body. I don't want to make him uncomfortable or nervous.

"Good morning." Adam finally exhales then flips around so he's facing me.

With both of his hands tucked under his pillow, he looks so sweet. Content. I can't help but smile.

"What?" A shy grin covers his face, lighting up his turquoise eyes. They look even brighter in the morning, although the genuinely happy smile he's presenting probably has something to do with that too.

"It's just fun to wake up to your smiling face."

Adam turns his head into the pillow for a few seconds then turns back to me, obviously trying to hide his joy at my approval. "Well, you can thank your boyfriend for that."

"Speaking of my boyfriend..." I wad up my pillow and tuck it lower under my neck so I'm elevated a little, looking down on Adam. "What were the sequence of events that led him to tucking you into bed with me?"

"Are you mad?" Adam asks quietly, genuinely worried.

"Of course not." I reach out and rest my palm on his small but firm bicep. "I'm happy, just a little surprised."

"I was too." Adam shrugs one shoulder. "I made him breakfast but he had to go to work. I guess he felt bad about leaving me down there alone so he asked if I wanted to lay with you."

"That sounds like Steve," I say tenderly, thinking of my compassionate and trusting lover. "He's amazing like that."

"He really is." Adam flips onto his back and stares at the ceiling. "You don't know how lucky you are."

"I think I do." I flip onto my back too, stretching my left arm and right leg, then twisting into a horizontal reverse warrior pose.

"I mean it, Joe. Most guys like Steve...." His voice trails off for a second as he rolls away from me, now facing the window. "Well, they're not like Steve. He's special. Don't let him go."

Adam's breathing is slow and measured, like he's trying to maintain his composure.

Moving only my arm, I reach out and place a hand on Adam's head, palming it like a basketball. Steve used to do this to me when I was feeling anxious or worried and it always made me feel better. Grounded. Owned.

After just a few slow breaths, Adam seems relaxed again. I remove my hand and sit up with my back facing him. I'm wearing boxers and a t-shirt but I've got a piss boner that won't quit.

"Let's get dressed and we can figure out something fun to do today."

~**~

"Okay." I grab my keys as Adam holds the garage door open for me. "Gym first then Target and the Waffle Haus. Is that it?"

"Yup." Adam pops the last bite of toast into his mouth as he bounds down the steps to my Escape.

"And we're just picking up your stuff at the gym? You don't want to work out?"

"Yeah." He shuts the car door behind him then waits for me to get into the driver's seat. "Tami probably thinks I'm dead so I need to let her know I'm fine and pick up my bag. I shouldn't be taking up a locker if I don't need to."

"And then Target?"

Adam shifts in the seat and turns to look out the window. "Yeah. I need to pick up a few new shirts if I'm going to be job hunting. I can't wear my catering uniform every day."

I smile to myself and pull out of the garage, proud at how far Adam has come in the week since I found him in the park. He is healthy, happy and looking forward to the future. Things are good.

By the time we run our errands and get to the Waffle Haus, Steve is taking off his apron. He gently scoots Brittney from the window when he hears me say hi to her.

"Did you finally figure out how to clone yourself, Joey?" The funky coed that had been managing this cart for the past six months loves to tease me about being Steve's houseboy.

"Maybe." I tease her back, putting my arm around Adam. "But this one doesn't play nicely with girls either. Sorry, babe."

"Of course not. The good ones never do!" Brittney scrunches up her nose then turns to the beeping waffle ovens.

Adam looks me over and smirks. "Clones?"

I take a quick look at him from head to toe. There is a definite resemblance. We are both right around 5'11". My chest and biceps are a bit thicker than Adam's still developing body but we could be brothers. My light blond hair is cut short, just long enough to cover my eyes. Adam's brown hair was shaved when I saw him on New Year's Eve but it has grown into shaggy waves over the past month. And his bright teal eyes run circles around my pale blue, almost clear ones. If we are clones, he is definitely the perfect original and I'm the slightly deformed copy.

"I don't know." I look up into Steve's adoring eyes. "What do you think, Ace? Could we be clones?"

"Nah." Steve shakes his head. "Not clones but definite compliments of each other. Like yin and yang. A complete package."

"What does that make you?" Adam asks quietly, his teeth tightly gripping his lower lip.

"One lucky bastard." Steve winks at Adam and releases him of his tension. Looking at me, he nods his head to the side of the small trailer. "Come on back."

While trying to stay out of the way, I give Adam the nickel tour, pointing out how the waffles are made and some of the delicious dips and toppings Steve has concocted. Adam's eyes are wide and he practically glows with excitement at each new thing he discovers in the 8x10 box trailer. "This is so cool!"

"It is!" I agree, watching proudly as Steve sprinkles rock salt on a caramel covered waffle. "He's amazing."

Steve grabs a cinnamon sugar waffle and hands it to me. "Thanks, Ace." Then Steve offers the salted caramel to Adam. "You wanna try my newest flavor?"

Adam reaches for the plate, but Steve pulls it back just a few inches. "What's the magic word?"

"Oh, um, please?" Adam straightens his back and drops his hand to his side like he's a solider at attention.

Steve smiles broadly and ruffles Adam's hair. "Here ya go, sweetie."

"Thank you." Adam blows out a breath then inhales the sweet and salty aroma coming from his plate. "This smells delicious."

"It is," Brittney and I say at the same time.

Steve leans on the counter between me and Adam. "So, what brings my favorite guys downtown?"

I love that Steve has been so accepting of Adam. It would have killed me to send him away when he was in such a bad situation. But, if Steve had one jealous or cruel bone in his body, that's probably what I would have had to do by now.

I never expected Steve to be so caring and gentle with Adam, giving him the same kind words and firm reassurances that he gives me. Okay, not exactly the same. But the same as when he first met me. Before we kissed or had sex. When he was just a stranger that picked up some kid from the streets and loved him unconditionally.

I want that for Adam too. In moments like this, I imagine what it would be like for the three of us to be together. Like really together. I'd never bring that up to Steve because he might think I was choosing

Adam over him. But I'm not. I could never choose anyone over Steve. He's my entire world. But since Adam has come back, he's managed to carve out a section of my heart that I wish I could offer him. He needs the love that I once gave him. The love Steve could give him. I'd never choose Adam over Steve. But, if given the option, I'd choose all of us.

Chapter Twelve

Adam

"Joey took me to pick up my stuff and I really wanted to see this place."

"Well, what do you think?"

Steve leans forward and opens his mouth over my plate. I have a piece of my waffle on a fork but I'm not sure what to do. A quick glance at Joey's amused face tells me to just go with it. So I do.

I slowly move the fork to Steve's mouth and watch as his teeth close over it. He pulls back slowly, his eyes burning a hole into me but I don't dare take my eyes off his mouth. I've imagined feeling that mouth on me so many times. Not just on my head or cheek, but really on me.

Kissing me. Licking me. Sucking me.

It takes me a few seconds to realize I'm still staring at his now smirking lips. Instinctively, I drop my chin to my chest, unable to make eye contact with either man.

Steve turns so he's facing us then places one hand on Joey's knee and one on mine. "Brittney can close up so I was just gonna head home. You guys have more errands to run?"

I shake my head and glance at Joey. "I'm all done."

"Me too." Joey is all smiles, though I'm not sure what has him in such a good mood. "Oh, actually, I was gonna stop by the store. Steve, can Adam ride home with you?"

"Of course." Steve steps between Joey's knees and pulls him into the kind of kiss I can only watch for a few seconds. It's like porn, sexy as fuck and making me hard. But I'm afraid if I don't look away, I might force myself between them, inserting myself somewhere I definitely don't belong. Uninvited and unwelcome, at least in these intimate moments.

I stand up and take a few steps toward the front window. There is a crowd of about six people waiting for Brittney to hand their waffles through the glass window.

Having a little store like this is my dream. I never considered waffles but I've always wanted to feed people, offering them joy and nourishment created from my own two hands.

I'm startled by Joey's arms closing around me. "I'll see you in a little bit. Okay, honey?" He's speaking quietly in my ear but I'm sure Steve can hear.

"Yeah, I'm good. Thanks." I hold Joey for just a second longer than I probably should, especially with Steve just inches behind me. I know I need to restrain myself better but I just can't help it. They both make me do things—want things—I can't have. People I can't have.

Joey pulls back and shocks the hell out of me when his lips skate over mine in a chaste kiss. I can't breathe until Steve's large hand settles on the small of my back. "Let's get home before it starts raining again. It looks like another storm is rolling in."

My eyes are wet but my cheeks aren't, so I nod and allow Steve to guide me to his truck. Once we're on the road, I find the nerve to ask the question that's been on my mind since I first saw the Waffle Haus.

"Um, Steve?"

His hand moves from the steering wheel and closes over my fist in the center console. "Yes."

"I, uh, noticed there was a help wanted sign at your store."

His hand doesn't move from mine like I expect. Instead, his grip tightens, holding me securely. "Yeah, I need someone to cover the weekends and a few afternoon shifts so I don't have to be there as often."

"Would you..." I don't know how to ask him. He knows I need a job. Why hasn't he asked me already? Maybe he doesn't want to hire me and is trying to spare my feelings. "Um, never mind."

Steve's grip on my hand tightens again, but this time it isn't in a comforting manner. He is trying to convey a message with his firm grip.

"Adam?" His voice is several octaves lower than it has been all day. He's not fucking around. "What are you trying to ask me?"

I close my eyes and blurt it out. "Would you consider hiring me? I swear I know how to make waffles and

I'll be good with customers. I even have some ideas for other dipping sauces you might want to try."

Steve's grip loosens and his palm slides up my arm then back down to my hand. "Thank you for being brave, sweetheart."

My eyes pop open and I turn to Steve. "Brave how?"

"By asking for what you want. You were afraid, but you fought through your discomfort and asked anyway. I'm proud of you."

My lips curl into a smile that covers my face. "Thank you, sir."

"But the reason I haven't asked you if you were interested is because I'm looking for someone to work during the times Joey is at home so I can spend more time with him." Steve's finger catches my chin and tugs it so I'm looking right at him. "And you. If you're working on the weekends, that defeats the purpose of trying to spend time together."

"You want..." I don't even know how to respond. I hear his words but I can't make sense of them. Is he saying...? "I mean, you want to spend time with me too? Not just Joey?"

Steve pulls my hand to his mouth and kisses the back of my hand softly. "Yes, Adam. Joey and I both want to spend time with you. We care about you and enjoy having you around."

"Oh." My chest is ready to burst with the joy it's trying to contain. I don't know how this could be happening but it's exactly what I've wanted since I first met Steve and Joey. I don't know where it'll lead but if they want to spend time with me, I want to be available.

But, I still have to work. I can't just sit around the house all day while Steve and Joey are gone. I'm feeling good now and it's time to earn my keep.

"Is that okay?" Steve asks as we turn onto his street.

"Yeah, of course," I say, almost sorry this car ride is over. It's one of the best of my life and I don't want the moment to end. "But, um, I still need a job. I guess I can keep looking for something part time."

When we pull into the garage, it takes me a minute to open the door and get out. Apparently that's a minute too long because Steve is standing over me when I look up. "Sweetheart, I've already asked you to say what you're thinking. I know you're thinking hard about something and I'll be wondering about it until you finally come clean." He steps back and gives me space to stand up. "Come on, show an old man some mercy and just fess up now."

"You are not an old man." I chuckle and walk into the kitchen. "You're—"

Holy shit. I almost said something stupid. What am I thinking? I turn toward the cabinet and pull out a glass, quickly filling it with water and hoping he hasn't heard me.

"I'm what?" Steve asks, sitting at the kitchen table.

I slide the glass in front of Steve then turn back to get one for myself. "Perfect," I whisper.

"I'm not perfect." Steve's voice is low and even but not angry, at least not that I can tell. "But you're the second person to mistake me for such."

I slowly approach the table and slip into the chair next to Steve. "Who was the first?"

"The man you're in love with."

"What?" I want to deny it, to tell Steve it's not true. But can't lie to him. I don't even try.

"It's okay, Adam." Steve hooks his foot around the wooden chair and pulls me closer. "I know you still love him. And I think he loves you too."

My head starts shaking uncontrollably. "No, no. No, Steve. He doesn't. He loves you." I stand up and head toward my room. "I'm sorry if I made you think otherwise. I shouldn't be here. I'm sorry."

Steve's thick, tatted up arm closes around my chest and pulls me back. I'm off my feet and pressed against Steve's firm body before I reach the hallway. "You're not leaving us, Adam. We want you here."

"But—"

"No buts. I'm not angry with you or Joey. I know he loves me and always will. But, he has room in his heart for both of us."

"He does?" Tears are streaming freely now and I don't try to hide them. I can't interrupt what he's saying. It's too important.

"Yes, sweetheart. He does." Steve's other arm closes across my chest and he rocks me a little. "And so do I. It's okay."

I don't know how to respond so I just lean against Steve's chest and cry. And he lets me.

Chapter Thirteen

Steve

Adam and I are still standing in the kitchen when Joey walks in. He's carrying a grocery bag that he drops on the table and rushes to us. "Is everything okay?"

I pull Joey into our little group hug and rest my forehead against his. "Is it, Adam?"

Adam nods. "If you say it is."

Joey's eyebrows furrow and he pulls away to look at Adam's face. With gentle fingers, he brushes away the few teardrops still streaking his cheeks. "What's wrong, honey? Please tell me."

115

Adam sniffs then inhales a shuddering breath. "Steve said." His whispered words trail off so I rub my palm over his chest, hoping to encourage him to keep going.

"What did Steve say?" Joey's eyes flick to mine for reassurance that I'm not upset. I smile and lean forward just far enough to kiss the tip of his nose.

Adam's heavy breathing quickens so I turn and place a soft kiss on his cheek. "Sweetheart, Joey and I have no secrets. Anything I say to you, you can say to him. I want you to always be honest with us."

"Steve said you love me." Adam turns his head away from Joey as soon as the words slide off his tongue.

Joey's gaze locks on mine for a full minute as we communicate without words. We need to have a conversation privately but I know it's true and Joey hasn't had the words to say it directly to me.

After finally finding the answers he's looking for in my expression, Joey scoots in front of Adam and holds his face in both hands. "I do love you, Adam. A part of me always has."

Adam falls into Joey's arms. I release him, giving them a moment before I wrap my arms around them both.

"So, what did you get at the store?"

Joey's eyes light up. "Champagne. The good kind."

"Nice." I pull two bottles out of the paper bag. There is also a cardboard container of melting chocolate and a basket of strawberries. "What are we celebrating?"

"Just us," Joey says, wrapping his arms around my waist and resting on my back. "It's been such a great day so far, I wanted to do something special."

"Sounds great, little duck." I pull his hands away and kiss each palm before turning in his arms. Without conscious thought, I take his mouth in a hot kiss. My lips cover his for just a few seconds but they're filled with so much heat that if we don't stop now, Adam will get an eyeful.

I reluctantly pull away and turn to the dishwasher. Putting away dishes is the perfect distraction. Mindless tasks always help me focus when things get crazy.

Living with two gorgeous men is definitely crazy.

At that thought, my cock begins to stiffen. I've certainly had my share of three-ways and Joey and Adam participated in group sessions when they were living at Paddles. But Joey and I have never talked about trying one together.

Honestly, I've never been interested in bringing in a third. I don't need or want any distraction from Joey and he hasn't expressed any interest in sharing our bed.

But that was before Adam. Everything has changed since Adam arrived. Not in a bad way, but I can feel the love Joey and Adam share. It's not as intense as what Joey and I have but it could be. If we nurture it and allow it to grow, it could be just as strong. And the more time I spend with these two beautiful men, the more I want to try it.

I already care deeply for Adam as a friend, and every time I see him smile lovingly at Joey, his place in my heart grows just a little bit more. Not pushing Joey out. Just more space being created.

At first, the idea scared me. When I met Adam at the wedding, I felt jealous of their history, and for the first time since we got together, I worried Joey might want Adam instead of me.

But once I saw how Joey interacted with him, I knew I didn't have to worry. Joey has the same strong need to take care of others that I have.

Actually, that's not true. Joey's is much stronger. I just want to take care of him. He wants to take care of the world. That's why he is so happy at the Pot of Gold.

"May I?" Adam's soft voice breaks me out of my daydream. He's holding up the basket of strawberries and the chocolate. "Or are we saving this for later?"

"No time like the present." I look around the room. "Where did Joey go?"

"He went up to take a shower. He said he'll be down in a few minutes."

I nod then adjust my hard-on. A shower sounds perfect. "I'm gonna run up too." I point at the food in his hands. "You got this?"

"Of course."

Spinning on my heels, I take the staircase three at a time, pulling my shirt over my head as I walk through the bedroom door. Just as my jeans hit the floor, Joey walks out of the bathroom with a billow of steam haloing his body and a towel tied around his delicious hips.

"You're done already?" I'm disappointed that I missed a chance at water sex. We haven't had a lot of shared showers lately.

"Yeah, sorry." His eyes darken as he stalks to me. He's not sorry at all. "I just needed to rinse off."

"Why didn't you ask me to join you?" I say in mock disapproval.

"Well, Adam was right there. I didn't want to make him uncomfortable."

I run a thumb across Joey's left nipple then glide over his chest to his right side. "Why didn't you ask him to join too?"

Joey inhales deeply. "Don't tease me, Ace. It's not nice."

"I'm not teasing, baby." I pinch his puckered skin then trail one finger down the center of his belly until it dips between the towel and his smooth pelvis. "I told you I'd give you anything you want. Anything you need."

"That includes another man?" Joey asks, confusion lacing his voice.

"Not just any other man." A drop of water falls from a lock of his baby fine hair and lands on his shoulder. I lean forward and catch it with the tip of my tongue then drag it up to his ear. "But Adam is different. If you want him in our shower, or our bed, I'm okay with that."

"You mean it? It won't change anything between me and you?"

The fact that he has to ask pisses me off. "Of course not." I step back and hold his face so he's looking straight at me. "I love you, Joey. I'll always love you. Nothing, and no one, can come between us. Do you feel the same way about me?"

Joey nods as tears fill his eyes. "Yes, Steve. You know that. You don't have to ask."

"Okay, then. It doesn't matter who else is a part of our life. We'll always have each other. No matter what."

"Yes, Ace. Always." Joey buries his nose in my neck and inhales. "No matter what."

An overwhelming urge to claim Joey fills me. I need to remind him that I love him and he loves me. I need him to feel me loving him, not just hear the words. I need my love for him to drip out of his ass for the rest of the day. Reminding him over and over just how good my love for him feels.

With one flick of my finger, the towel around Joey's waist is gone and we're both naked and horny. Joey must recognize the beast just below the surface because he takes one look at my face and hops on the bed. His feet are perched at the side with his open ass presented to me as a beautiful gift. Not even a bow could make this picture prettier.

Joey doesn't wait for me to grab the lube before he buries one finger in his hole and starts fucking himself, stretching his tight muscle so he can take me all the way in.

I'm not capable of making love right now. The primal urge in my body will not be sated by slow and easy. I need to fuck. Hard. And Joey needs it too. I squirt a trail of slick on my cock and stroke it once while Joey fucks three fingers on his right hand.

"I'm ready, Ace." Joey's already panting. His dick is hard but not leaking yet. "Fuck me."

"Whatever you ask for, baby." I stroke down my cock one more time then lock my thumb over the base of my cock to guide it home. My other fingers gently pulse against my balls as I push into Joey's ass with a slightly wet sound. He used enough saliva on himself that I probably didn't need the lube but I'm grateful for it. "Fuck, you feel so good."

"You feel better, Ace. Go fast. I want it fast."

Moving my hand from my balls to Joey's, I gently finger them while plowing into him. His dick is fully hard and a drop of come is begging for me to taste it. I don't want to break my rhythm so I use a finger to steal away the seed and spread it across my tongue. "You're the most delicious dessert I've ever tasted."

Joey grabs two pillows and shoves them under his lower back so I'm at a better angle. The right angle to press into his happy spot with every thrust. My bed is high enough to fuck next to but Joey likes to really feel the burn when we've had an emotional or upsetting conversation. Right now, he needs me to get rough. No coddling or slow movements. He doesn't want soothing words or gentle touching. He wants me to bury my dick to the hilt into his sore and raw ass until he spews out all the tension and nervous energy he's currently harboring.

Never one to deny my little duck, I push harder. Faster. My balls pull tight and I lean completely over Joey, using gravity to get me as deep as I can go.

"Oh, god. Steve!" I wrap one hand around Joey's cock as his fingers move to his nipples. He tweaks while I pull. He pulls while I twist. "Fuck!"

Joey shoots two thick ropes of come across his belly and chest. He's created a work of art without even realizing it. But I realize it and appreciate the exceptional beauty in seeing the man I love covered in his own come after I've ridden him hard. My own release comes quickly, starting in my belly and shooting endorphins and tranquility from my toes to my nose.

I could never give him up. I never will. And I know Joey feels the same way.

CHAPTER FOURTEEN

ADAM

I know what they're doing. When Steve rushed upstairs at the mention of Joey in the shower, it was pretty obvious what was coming next. But that doesn't stop me from heading up the stairs once the sounds of their writhing become loud enough to cover the two squeaky steps.

I just want to watch. Just once. I need to see for myself that they're real. That what they have is real. Honestly, it's hard to believe they're so perfect together all the time. As much of an asshole as it makes me, I'm almost hoping to find some fault in their relationship. Something that makes them more real.

More *normal.*

But when I'm high enough on the stairs that I can peek over the landing into their bedroom, what I see isn't normal. It's nothing like anything I've experienced, not even when I was with Joey myself, back in the day.

This is beautiful. Magical. Steve pushing and Joey pulling in perfect harmony. Their bodies know each other well enough to respond in a way that draws maximum pleasure from the other. Joey bucks, just as Steve thrusts. Steve strokes Joey's cock as Joey pinches his own nipples.

I don't know when my hand slid inside my pants, but when Joey sprays a thick stream of come on his chest, I feel my own release coat my hand.

Shit. I shouldn't be here. I shouldn't be watching this. Watching them.

I lean forward so my head isn't sticking up from the second story floor before I take a step forward. With the squeaky boards, I don't want to be caught peeping.

Once I'm at the bottom step, I take a quick breath. "The strawberries are ready. I'm gonna take a quick shower too."

"Be right down," Joey calls in a sleepy voice.

~**~

My skin is still pink and moist from the scalding hot shower when I step into the living room. Steve and Joey are on the floor with a tray of chocolate dipped strawberries and three champagne flutes between them.

They both look up at me with content smiles when I approach. "Come." Joey pats the empty space between him and Steve. "I'm dying to try these."

"Oh, you shouldn't have waited," I say as I cross my ankles and drop down onto the area rug. The fireplace is glowing with a stack of cedar logs that crackle every few seconds. The scene is straight out of a romantic movie.

Steve hands me and Joey a glass then reaches for his own. "To fresh starts and finding happiness, no matter how unconventional it might look."

"Cheers!" Joey has a conspiratorial smile on his face that makes me cock an eyebrow. He ignores my unspoken question and nods toward my glass.

"Cheers," I say, clinking against their sparkling crystal. I down half the glass in one gulp. It's not

Aria Grace

classy but I need to calm my nerves. The shower helped but now that I'm sitting so close between the two men that I was spying on just minutes ago, I feel anxious. Afraid they know what I've done.

"These strawberries look so good, Adam." Joey grabs one and smells it. "And they smell so good." Instead of taking a bite, he holds it out to Steve.

Steve leans forward and bites the tip off. "Mmm, it tastes even better."

I'm hypnotized by the way Steve's mouth closes over the dessert. He savors the taste, keeping his eyes locked on Joey's. But now they're locked on me. I'm startled to realize I've been caught staring. Then I realize why. Joey is holding the rest of the strawberry in front of my mouth.

"Try it, honey. You deserve the second bite since you made them."

Holding Joey's gaze, I lean forward just an inch and open my mouth. He meets me the rest of the way, moving the strawberry to my lips. Without blinking, I bury my teeth into the soft fruit. Sweet and tangy juices flood my senses. Fuck, I never knew strawberries could be so good.

Steve groans quietly beside me but I don't look away as Joey pops the rest into his mouth and bites it down to the stem. "Mmm, perfect."

"Yes, this is," Steve whispers, reading my mind.

We spend the next few minutes quietly enjoying the warmth of the fire and the crisp champagne. Just as my thoughts begin to wander to what I witnessed upstairs, Steve pulls me out of my memories.

"Adam?"

"Yes, sir?" I look him straight in the eye, shoulders squared and respectful.

"When we got home, there was something you wanted to say but didn't. Do you remember what it was?"

I think back to our conversation about the job opening at Waffle Haus. My facial expression must have changed because the corners of Steve's mouth pull up. "Good. What was it?"

"Oh." I reach for a strawberry and wave away the question. "It wasn't anything important."

"Adam." Steve's voice is low and commanding. I can't help the shiver that vibrates down my spine.

Staring at my strawberry, I resolve to not be such a fucking pussy around him. If I want Steve to respect me, and Joey for that matter, I need to stop being a baby and just speak freely.

"I was just thinking that I'd really love to work for you. I know what you said about nights and weekends, but maybe if you have a day time opening in the future, I hope you'll consider me."

Steve smiles proudly and places his hand on my knee. "Are you sure you wouldn't rather work in a restaurant or somewhere with a more diversified menu? Something you can really learn from."

I shake my head emphatically, probably too emphatically by the way Steve's eyes twinkle in the firelight. "What you've created, that's my dream. I've always wanted to open my own business. Something small. Just like your store. I know I could learn so much from you."

"Thank you for telling me what you want, sweetheart." Steve squeezes my knee. "It would be nice to spend more time with you. We can get to know each other better and I really need the help."

"Really?" I'm holding my breath, waiting to see if he means what I think he means.

"Yes, Adam. I'd love to have you come work with me."
I finally release the oxygen from my lungs and jump
up on my knees, throwing my arms around Steve's
neck and falling into his chest.

"Thank you, thank you!" I screech into the side of his
head. "I promise I won't let you down."

"I know, sweetie." Steve rubs my back with his wide
hands, filling me with security and joy. "I'll need
more help at the kiosk in a few months so I can train
you part time for now and we'll go from there. If you
want more or less hours, we'll make it work."

When I sit back down, I look over at Joey. "Oh, is that
okay with you?"

He holds his arms open and I fly into them with as
much enthusiasm as I had for Steve. "Of course it's
okay. I think it's a great idea."

Chapter Fifteen

Joey

The rest of weekend is chill. We play games, cook meals, and just spend time together. Steve and I drop little hints and innuendo about Adam being a more permanent member of our family but we're taking things slow.

Adam needs time to get to know us and we need to get to know him. Inviting him into our relationship is a big step. A crazy step. Not something I would have considered with anyone other than Steve. Or Adam. But something about the idea feels right. And when the timing is also right, we'll make a go of it.

"Joey!" Bryce calls from downstairs. "Can you come down here?"

I've been back at the Pot of Gold full-time for a week now and things are just as hectic as ever. The weather has cleared up so we actually have empty beds right now but there's always drama in the after school rec room we've set up in the basement. As a kid, having free rein in a room full of video games, candy dispensers, and cable TV would have kept me quiet for hours. But, inevitably, we have to calm some kind of disturbance at least once a day.

"I told him to stop and he wouldn't." I can hear Jorge's pissed off shouts before I hit the bottom step. "It's his own damn fault."

Bryce is holding Jorge by his shoulders to keep him away from Woo. Woo has only been coming here for a few days but he quickly formed an attachment with Bobby, our resident mute. Bobby doesn't talk, but he's a sweet kid that likes to help out around here.

He'll clean up after everyone leaves and he's the first to volunteer for kitchen duty when Mamma Ria can't come in to cook for us.

By the way Woo is holding his jaw, and Bobby is staring wide-eyed from the farthest corner of the basement, I get a pretty good idea of what's going on.

"Woo, with me." I point to the staircase. He slowly turns to me and walks up. Looking back at Bryce, I cock an eyebrow. "You good?"

He smiles. "Oh, we're good. In fact, I think Jorge and I are going for a little run while we talk. What do you say, kid?" He turns to a confused Jorge. "Maybe eight miles? Or should we go for an even ten?"

Jorge rolls his eyes but doesn't argue. No one argues with Bryce. He's one of the nicest guys I've met but his tall, muscular frame is intimidating as hell.

I laugh to myself as I climb the stairs, guiding Woo into my office. Once we're both seated, I give him a minute to gather his thoughts. When it's clear he isn't going to speak first, I clear my throat to get his attention.

"Okay, kid. What happened?"

He shrugs. "Jorge hit me. Popped me in the jaw for no reason."

"No reason?" I smirk, knowing exactly what the reason was, but needing him to admit it. "Really?"

"What?" Woo slouches down in the chair so his shoulders box in his ears. "I was just talking to Bobby. Seeing if I could get him to talk, you know?"

"Did he?" I pick up a pencil from the desk and roll it over my fingers. I've learned this is a great distraction tactic. The person sitting across from me can't help but to watch as the pencil flips over and under each of my knuckles. They always spill their guts without even realizing it.

"Hmm?" Woo pulls his gaze away from my hand long enough to catch my eye. "No, not really. But he smiled. And I think he was going to reach for my hand."

"So why was Jorge pissed?"

"You know why, man. He has a thing for Bobby. He's just too much of a pussy to say anything. I'm not gonna sit on my ass and wait. I decided to make my move."

I stop the pencil and hold it between both hands. "I'm not sure Bobby's ready for you to make a move, man. Maybe you should back off for a little while and give him time to get to know you."

"Nah." Woo scoots to the edge of the chair and puts his elbows on his knees. "We done here? I asked Bobby to help me with calculus."

"Do you need help?" I ask. "Because Kim is really good with math. She can help if you need it."

Woo laughs. "Dude, look at my eyes. I'm Chinese. I've been doing calculus since I was eight. I'm just trying to get close to him."

I smirk and toss the pencil at him. "Just take it easy with that kid. And try not to go to blows with Jorge. He has a protective side that you don't want to cross."

"Yeah, yeah." Woo stands up. "So I can go?"

I wave my hand toward the door. "Go already!"

My phone rings as Woo disappears. A picture of Steve's sexy chest lights up the screen. I want to taste those nipple rings, tugging them between my teeth until he's begging for mercy. Or release. Or both.

"Hey, Ace. How's work going?"

"Great." Steve always sounds happy to hear my voice at the end of the day. It makes my belly warm just knowing how much he love me. "We're gonna pick up dinner on the way home. Is Chinese good?"

"Sounds great. I'm almost done here too. I'll be home by seven."

"Drive safely, baby."

"You too."

Since Adam started helping out at the cart, Steve has been much more relaxed. I know they have fun together and the taste testing Adam asks me to participate in every morning is just gravy. I've probably gained five pounds in the past week that they've been working together.

When I get home, the coffee table is covered in takeout boxes and Steve and Adam are leaning against the couch, watching a Blazers Raptors game. "Who's winning?" I ask as I hang my jacket on a hook by the door.

"Raptors by eight." Steve hits the mute button on the remote as I approach. His arms open and I drop into his lap, just wanting to be held. "How was your day, little duck?"

"Fine but I'm glad to be home."

Steve's arm close around me and hold tightly. "We're glad you're home too."

My mouth is drawn to Steve's almost magnetically. Resting my lips on his, I nip and tug then drag my tongue between his teeth and the silky inside of his lip. That always drives him crazy.

Steve's fingers dig into my ass, kneading through my jeans as I rock into his crotch. When we come up for air, I open my eyes and see Adam watching us. He's only inches away from us but it's still too far.

His eyes are wide and his pupils big. Even his breaths sound like he was part of that kiss.

I take one more nibble of Steve's lip then look into his eyes. "I love you."

"I love you too, baby." He nods once, giving me the permission I'm seeking.

I pull back just a few inches and turn to Adam.

"Come here, you."

With lustful eyes, Adam closes the distance between us. My hand wraps around his neck and I pull him to me, taking his mouth in a gentle kiss.

His lips are parted, probably from shock, but I don't take advantage of it. I just lick them, tugging his lower lip with my teeth then tracing it with my tongue. "Did you have a good day, honey?"

"Uh huh." His lids are drooping like he's in a daze. "The best."

"I'm happy to hear that." I pat the back of his neck then turn to the food on the table. "Did you guys eat yet? I'm starving."

Steve's finger is rubbing figure eights on my back. "No, baby. We wanted to wait for you."

I cock an eyebrow at Steve in a suggestive way. "I'm glad you didn't start without me."

Steve's hand drops down to my ass and he squeezes. "It's a good thing you weren't much later or we might have."

Adam squeaks from beside us, probably wondering if we're still talking about food. Actually, he's not stupid. He knows we were never talking about food.

Chapter Sixteen

Steve

How did I get so lucky? Someone upstairs must have made a clerical error on the list of good fortune, because there is no way I deserve everything I have.

Joey is the love of my life. The reason I wake up every morning. The playful side to my gruff exterior. The light to my darkness. And now we have Adam to round us out. Excitable but insecure. Ambitious yet humble. Damaged but healing.

Under my firm grasp, and Joey's constant encouragement, Adam is becoming the man he was meant to be. The man Joey loved so many years ago. The man I'm starting to feel that same love for.

Working together was the right move for us. Adam isn't nervous or afraid of me anymore. Whoever hurt him in the past really messed with his mind. Adam looked at me with fear in his eyes when he first showed up, convinced I'd be disappointed in him and punish him the way others had in his past. But that's not how he looks at me now.

Adam's eyes are smoldering with only a thin rim of turquoise surrounding heated black. He is ready. Ready for Joey to kiss him again. And ready for me to touch him for the first time.

Not a friendly or concerned touch, but a sensual touch. The touch of a lover. And after tonight, I hope that's what we'll be. The three of us learning to love each other as we explore the facets of our hearts and souls.

"Ace?" Joey palms my cheek and I lean into it, looking into his eyes. "You hungry? Or should I put the food in the fridge for now?"

"I'm starving." I turn into his hand, nipping at his fingertips. "So you better put the food away."

Adam and Joey both rush to clean up the food that will have to be reheated later.

I can't wait. I need them. Both of them.

When they return, I've moved the coffee table out of the way and turned off the TV. The only light is from a dim table lamp and the crackling fire behind me.

Lifting a hand out to each man, I guide them to kneel in front of me. I'm sitting on my ass with my legs crossed so we're all at equal height.

"Adam, sweetheart." My voice is raspy as I run my fingers through is shaggy hair, closing my hand around his nape. "Joey and I want to love you. We want to make love to you. Is that okay?"

Adam chokes out a sob and nods his head. "Yes, please. Please touch me."

Grasping both his shoulders, I pull Adam and lift him so he's straddling my lap. Joey quickly moves in behind him, rubbing his neck for reassurance.

With both my hands now holding his face, I tilt Adam's head to the side and kiss him gently. It's the first time my lips have tasted him in a sexual way. He's delicious and so receptive to my touch, immediately opening his mouth and granting me access to his greedy tongue.

I sweep my tongue over his, but Adam wants more. He sucks my tongue into his mouth and fucks it. The wet, sloshy noises instantly make me hard.

Reaching one hand blindly back, I hold on to Joey's neck and pull him closer. His chin is almost resting on Adam's neck when I pull away to take Joey's mouth in mine. The two men taste different but are equally addicting. I kiss Joey like a soldier coming home from war, while my other hand slides beneath Adam's shirt.

My large hand slides across Adam's taut back. His skin is soft. I want to feel more of it. All of it. My pinkie dips below his waistband and teases the top of his crack. His teeth clamp on my neck for a second before he releases. It's fucking hot.

Joey pulls back and I yank Adam's shirt over his head just before Joey turns his head and takes his mouth. With both of my men occupied, I can do what I need to do. Take off their fucking clothes.

My hands move to Adam's jeans first, quickly releasing the button and zipper. Without letting go of Joey's mouth, Adam sits up on his knees so I can pull his jeans down below his ass. His cock is beautiful. It's absolutely sinful the way his slim rod curves left, directly toward Joey. I scoot back on my knees then bend to take him in my mouth. I can't wait a second longer to have his hard dick inside me.

Without wasting any time, I suck his head through my tightly pursed lips, as if he's breaching a different kind of pucker. Adam's chest expands as he inhales sharply. Joey's mouth moves to Adam's jaw and nibbles while he watches me suck Adam down my throat, until his soft brown curls are tickling my nose.

"Oh, god." Adam is bucking into me. "It feels so good, Steve."

Joey's hand slides below my chin, cupping Adam's tight balls and pulling them away from his body. "That's right, honey. Just enjoy it. Let Steve take care of you. Let us love you."

As soon as Joey lets the "L" word fly, Adam's body locks in an arched position and he shoots down my throat. It's been so long since I've tasted come that wasn't from Joey that I'm almost surprised when it's different. Not better or worse. Just different.

"Mmm." I hold a mouthful of his cream in my mouth and kiss Joey hard, sharing the bounty Adam has offered. "He's delicious, baby. Just like you."

Joey's tongue ravishes me, licking every crevasse. Stealing Adam's essence right from me. But that's okay. I know how to get more.

"That was so fucking hot, Ace." Joey's tongue trails from my jaw to my neck. "I want to watch you do that again. Every fucking day."

I smile and look over at Adam. "What do you think, sweetheart? Can Joey watch me do that every day?"

"Fuck yeah." His hand is slowly stroking his growing cock. This boy doesn't need much time to recover. That'll come in handy. Pun intended.

"Can I?" Joey asks quietly, looking from me to Adam. "You know, can I taste him too?"

We both look at Adam. His thumb and forefinger are locked around the base of his cock and his eyes are heavily lidded. "Please."

I nudge Adam into a lying position and Joey dive bombs onto his cock, licking the length from root to tip then sliding his tongue into the slit. Every swipe of his sensitive opening causes Adam to buck up off the ground.

After taking off my clothes, I slide in behind Adam, lifting his head so it's resting on my thigh. His cheek nuzzles my hard-on like it's a pillow. The top of Adam's nose runs the length, and his tongue shoots out now and then to steal a taste.

I think he wants more but he's not ready to take everything yet. And that's okay. We have plenty of time to try everything. Tonight is just about showing him that we want him in our life as more than just a roommate.

When Joey's hand wraps around his cock, I reach for his thigh and pull his body around so his cock is in Adam's face. Adam leans up on one elbow and tentatively lowers his mouth onto Joey's dick, softly licking and kissing my beautiful boy. Our beautiful boy.

When Adam's licking turns into sucking and Joey's balls are bathed in a stream of saliva, I take this as an opportunity to please my little duck. With one hand on Adam's hip, I'm simultaneously holding him up so he can reach Joey, and holding him down so Joey can reach him. I swirl the middle finger of my other hand through the pool of spit, taking a moment to fondle Joey's balls while I'm there. He moans, delving further onto Adam's cock and tilting up for me.

I know what he wants. What he needs. Sliding my finger to his pucker, I gently work my way in. My fingertip brushes over his prostate and Joey explodes. Shooting straight up in a fountain of creamy juice, he surprises Adam while he's tonguing Joey's balls.

"Fuck, Joey." Adam sucks Joey's head, slurping out the remaining drops. "I wanted that."

"I want some too, sweetheart. Get me a mouthful," I say to Adam.

Adam drags his tongue across Joey's belly and pulls the ribbon of seed into his mouth then turns to me. I take Adam's mouth forcefully, licking and sucking what I want straight off his tongue. Adam moans and his whole body locks up again, shooting into Joey's awaiting mouth.

When Joey is satisfied he's drawn every last drop from Adam's softening dick, Joey crawls up and shares the load with me. Tasting both men in my mouth is almost enough to make me shoot. Almost.

"Steve." Adam's sweet voice makes Joey smile. He backs away from my mouth and we pull Adam into our little huddle.

"Yes, sweetheart." I brush my stubbly cheek across his soft skin while Joey rubs a rogue drop of come over Adam's tip.

"Thank you."

With Adam's mouth on mine, I kiss him hard, letting him know I'm not doing him any favors. I want him. Joey wants him. He wants us. We need each other. This is how it should be. "Thank you for trusting us."

CHAPTER SEVENTEEN

ADAM

It's almost ten when we finally warm up the food and eat dinner. Conversation is a little awkward, even once we're dressed again, but I try not to let that worry me. I know Steve and Joey wouldn't have done something like that if their relationship couldn't handle it. I'd seen lots of relationships go bad when someone cheated but that's not what happened.

Steve and Joey both invited me to have an intimate night with them. That's all. They say they want it to be more, and I can't lie and say I don't want that to be true. But I'm a realist. I know how this works.

They'll let me play with them for a while, maybe even treat me like I'm an equal partner. But that will never be the case. I'll always be a third wheel. Their plus one for a good time. Until I become more of a burden than they're interested in and they send me on my way. Just like Lee did. And every man who came before him.

We're cuddled up on the couch, Joey on one side of Steve and me on the other, when I hear quiet snoring coming from the other side of the couch.

Steve and I both turn to see Joey's beautiful face, completely slack and angelic as he sleeps, curled up next to Steve's chest. I want to snap a picture but I'm too embarrassed to ask if it's okay.

Steve kisses my temple and pats my shoulder. "I should get him up in bed." I move out of his way so he can stand with Joey cradled in his big, tattooed arms. "I'll be right back."

While Steve is upstairs, I decide to go to sleep too. It's been a long day and I'm looking forward to sleeping in tomorrow. Brittney is opening the cart so Steve and I both have the day off.

Before heading to my room, I turn off the TV and make sure the front door is locked. I'm just slipping out of my clothes when Steve knocks on the open door.

"Adam, may I come in?"

My jeans are mid-thigh, but Steve has already seen everything so I let them fall to the floor then slide between the sheets. "Of course."

"I thought you might want to sleep upstairs with us tonight." He takes a few steps into the room but isn't close enough to touch.

"Oh, no, that's okay." I play it off like it doesn't matter to me. Like it isn't one of the things I want most in this world. "I'm fine in here."

"Are you sure?" Steve finally closes the distance between us and sits on the side of my bed, so we're hip to hip. "We'd love to have you there in the morning."

I smile at the memory of Joey saying something similar when he woke up to me in his bed. *Did he tell Steve about that comment?*

"Thanks, Steve. Really, I'm fine here." I slide down so I'm horizontal and pull the sheet up to my chin. "Besides, I like to stretch out so I'll be more comfortable here."

The look of disappointment on Steve's face is as shocking as it is heartbreaking. "Oh, well, okay. I won't push you to do anything you're not ready for."

I nod without speaking, unable to trust that my voice won't crack if I do.

"Adam?" Steve's voice is firm and my eyes immediately lock on his.

"Yes, sir."

"Are you okay with everything that happened tonight?"

I take a deep breath and steel my nerves. I will not cry. I will not cry. "Absolutely. It was amazing."

Steve nods then leans down to kiss me. His lips hold against mine for a second but then lift and move to my temple. "Sleep well, sweetheart."

"You too, Steve."

As Steve walks away, every fiber of my being wants to shout out for him to stop. Beg him to take me with him. Allow him to carry me upstairs and into his bed like he just did for Joey.

But I don't.

For the first time in a long time, I stay strong and do the right thing. I don't give in to temptation. I make the smart choice and stay in the guest room they've offered. One and a half more months. I should have enough money to move by then. I just hope they aren't sick of me before that happens.

~**~

Working with Steve is better than I thought it would be. The first week was mostly training. Then the second week was all about customer service and making sure everyone was happy with their waffles and willing to share their good experiences with friends.

But yesterday, Rachel slipped in the shower and had some spotting so her doctor ordered to stay in bed for at least three days. That leaves me to run the mall kiosk.

When I'm there alone, I can pretend I own the place. Like it's my little slice of capitalism that could give me the freedom and independence I've always wanted.

Back in Seattle, there was a guy I thought would be my first. He was older than me by at least ten years, but I learned a lot from Alex. He was the first man I knew that was openly gay. And he was awesome. Athletic. Funny. Hot as hell. If I was a few years older, or at least legal, I think something might have happened. But he eventually moved to Colorado and I was left with only assholes to torment me and selfish pricks as role models.

When I left Paddles, I considered contacting Alex. He worked at some fancy advertising agency and I thought maybe he could help me get a job out there. But when I looked him up on Facebook, I found a picture of him with some cowboy and a baby. I didn't want to mess anything up for them. Just like I won't mess anything up for Joey and Steve.

I'll work my ass off at the Waffle Haus and maybe Steve will let me run this one when Rachel goes on maternity leave. After that, I'll figure things out. I can't plan that far in advance. Life is too unpredictable to make plans a year or more into the future. I live for today and tomorrow. That's what has kept me going this far, and that's how I expect to continue.

Chapter Eighteen

Joey

After a few days of awkwardness, we've all settled into a good rhythm at home. Steve goes into work early and I drop Adam off at either shop when I head into the Pot.

We've had a sequence of heavy storms over the past two weeks, so a lot of new and familiar faces have been staying with us or just seeking a few hours of shelter.

I'd say things were great at home, but Steve and I haven't cracked the shell with Adam quite yet. Steve thinks maybe we misread his interest in a relationship. We've fooled around together a few times but nothing serious and no penetration.

Adam has always been funny about being fucked. Even back when he was a prostitute at Paddle's, he hated to be fucked. He did it because he had to, but he never let me near his ass. And he never wanted to get near mine. I've tried to talk to him about it but he just changes the subject.

I'm not convinced it's disinterest in a relationship. In fact, I think it's the opposite because I felt the same way when I first came to live with Steve. I couldn't believe a man like him would want a broken and beaten kid like me. He had so much to offer and I came with nothing. Penniless and enough emotional baggage to sink a ship.

But Steve was patient with me and we're both hoping the same tactic will work with Adam. We even have a little weekend getaway planned.

We're taking him to the beach on Saturday. February isn't traditionally the beach season in Oregon, but the ocean side bungalow we rented will be perfect for us to figure things out. Most importantly, we'll have the privacy to actually be together.

I'm vacuuming the entryway at the Pot when I hear frantic voices in the kitchen. Worried Kim might need some help, I rush through the swinging door to check on things.

"God, Joey. Did you hear?"

"Hear what?" I put my arm around her and let her cry on my shoulder. "They finally found Kurt. He OD'd a few days ago."

"Fuck." I close my other arm around Kim and hold her, letting her warm tears soak into my shirt while mine wet the side of her hair. "When did you hear?"

"Bryce just called. He got a call from the investigator we've been bugging." Her body shakes in quiet sobs. "God, I can't believe this happened."

I can't believe it either. We stopped looking for him a few weeks ago when his dealer told us Kurt left town. He said something about a sick grandma so we stopped worrying. Clearly, that was a mistake.

If we'd found him just a few days earlier, he might still be alive. I want to break something. Punch a hole in something. But Kim is in my arms and she needs me to be strong. I can comfort her in the way I've been trained.

And I'll get mine later. At home. From Steve. All I want is to let Steve hold me. Kiss me. Whisper sweet words that make my belly flutter and my dick hard. I just need to be with him.

For the next few hours, we break the news to everyone that knew Kurt and answer as many questions as we can. Unfortunately, there aren't many we can answer.

"His parents are planning a funeral for him on Saturday afternoon. The investigator said it's open to the public if we want to attend."

I nod and check my watch. "Yeah, I'll be there."

"Good." Kim gives me one more hug. "I want to go too, but I was afraid I wouldn't know anyone."

I rub my eyes, knowing they must be puffy and red. "I think I'm gonna head home. Is there anything you need before I go?"

"No, I'm fine." She runs her fingers through her long hair and wipes her hands on her leggings. "Thank you for being here for me. For all of us."

I offer a weak smile. "I'll see you tomorrow, Kim."

~**~

As usual, Steve and Adam aren't home when I get there. Instead of making something for dinner or snuggling on the couch while I wait, I head upstairs and climb into bed. I barely take off my shoes and jacket before pulling the thick comforter over my head and finally letting out the emotion I'm feeling. This isn't the first time we've lost someone at the Pot. It happens. Unfortunately, LGBT youth are at much greater risk for violent or drug related deaths, especially those living on the streets.

I don't know why I'm taking his loss so personally but I am. I feel like I failed Kurt. I had been out there looking for him. If I hadn't... Well, if I hadn't found Adam and gotten distracted by my past crush on him, I might have kept looking, even when everyone else had given up. I might have found him before it was too late.

I know it's not my fault, but that doesn't stop the tears from pouring down my cheeks in sheets and the full body sobs that rock the bed.

I don't know how much time has passed but Steve is home.

"Joey!" Steve yanks back the covers and pulls me into his arms. "Oh, god. Baby, what happened? Are you hurt?"

He's frantic, almost in tears himself as I shake my head, trying to control myself. "I'm fine. Steve. It's okay, I'm fine."

"You're not fine, Joey. What happened?"

I take a deep breath and hold my breath, trying to calm my convulsing lungs. "Kurt died. He overdosed a few days ago. He was still here the whole time, but we stopped looking and now he's dead. I shouldn't have stopped looking for him."

I bury my face in Steve's chest and let him work his magic. His strong arms cage me against his chest, reminding me that I'm his. Wholly and completely owned by this amazing man. He'll always protect what's his. Me. Adam. Our family. Everything.

I let his soothing voice lull me to sleep with promises of always being loved and cared for.

Chapter Nineteen

Adam

Steve was telling me about the tide pools we'd see at the beach this weekend when we walked into the dark house. The sound of Joey's tortured crying made me stop in my tracks.

All color drained from Steve's face as he dropped the bag of groceries he'd been holding and ran up the stairs. I followed behind, close but not too close. I was worried about Joey but also terrified of Steve.

I hadn't felt that kind of fear since I first met him. He looked murderous as he pulled Joey into his arms and inspected him for injury. If someone had hurt Joey, I felt sorry for them because they had a painful visit from Steve in their near future.

I stood at the foot of the bed as Joey choked out the words that made my blood run cold.

Kurt, the man Joey was looking for on the night he found me, was dead. Instead of continuing to look for him, and possibly finding him that night or any of the nights since then, Joey stopped searching. He brought me home and catered to me, as if I needed to be saved.

I wasn't any more important than this Kurt guy. He may have been a junkie, but Joey clearly cared about him. Cared enough to go looking for him in the middle of a storm.

Joey's words hang in the air like a wet fog. *I shouldn't have stopped looking for him.*

He blames himself. No, he probably blames me. It's my fault. I'm the one that moved into his house, tried to insert myself into his family. I've been creating distraction after distraction for over a month. If he never found me, he could have found Kurt. He could have saved this man that needed to be saved. A man worthy of saving.

Joey is curled into Steve as if he's trying to climb under his skin. Pain isn't only etched on Joey's porcelain features. It's also evident on Steve's strong face. Instead of the tough and in control man I've started to fall in love with, this man is tortured. His pain is almost as powerful as Joey's but instead of manifesting in tears and wails, Steve's pain is like a bubble just below the surface of his control. Pushing to escape but not finding an exit. Not yet, at least.

I can't watch this. I can't witness this anguish when I know it could have been avoided. If I wasn't such a burden on their lives over the past month, they might not be experiencing one of the worst moments of their lives.

I slowly back out of the room.

"Adam?" Steve's voice is like a growl and I almost whimper in response.

My heart is ready to beat out of my chest as I make eye contact. "Yes."

"Would you like to stay with us tonight? I'm sure Joey would appreciate having you here."

I shake my head. "I don't think I can help. You're better equipped to handle this stuff."

Steve looks confused by my answer but bounces his chin once in a slight nod. "I'll check on you later. Okay, sweetie?"

I smile at the endearment. Even with everything going on, all the pain that my presence in their life has caused, he can still call me sweetie.

I can't speak through the lump in my throat, so I just exit the room and walk down the stairs, leaving a trail of tears all the way to my bed.

~**~

Last night was rough. Every time Joey cried out in his sleep or whimpered for Steve, my resolve grew stronger. I can't keep up the charade any longer. I can't keep up the fantasy that I belong here. With them.

It's not fair to myself and it sure as fuck isn't fair to Joey or Steve.

They deserve to get their life back. The happy, uncomplicated life they were living before I was dragged in like a wet rat. That's essentially what I was. What I still am. Just a vile rodent that needs to be exterminated.

With the sun shining through the window, comes the clarity I need to move forward. I have a plan and I'm no longer afraid to do what needs to be done.

A sense of peace falls over me that I've never felt before. I've never known contentment as I do now that I know what my future looks like. Why didn't I think of this sooner? Why did I spend so many years running?

Hiding.

Fighting.

Hurting.

This is so much better. I feel...zen.

When Steve comes down at six thirty, I've got a bacon and cheese quiche in the oven and a pot of coffee waiting for him.

"Good morning," I say as I hand him the cup. "I hope you got some sleep last night."

Steve's eyes narrow for a second but the aroma from the steaming cup easily distracts him. "Thank you, sweetie. I needed this."

"Of course!" I check my watch and grab an oven mitt to pull the quiche out. "Breakfast will be ready in five minutes. Is Joey coming down?"

"Um, I'm not sure. He had a rough night," Steve says, now looking at me more closely. "What about you? How did you sleep?"

"Great." The look of surprise on Steve's face reminds me that last night was not a great night. "Well, not great, but I guess I slept well enough because I feel good. Are you going to work today or is Brittney filling in?"

"I'll have to call her but I'm sure she can cover for me. And if you want to stay home to be with Joey, that's fine. I have a few back up people, ex-employees, I can call if I need to."

"No, don't worry about it." I cut two slices of the warm quiche and put them on plates. "I don't know about you but I'm starving."

Steve is still watching me through narrowed slits when I slide his plate in front of him and sit down across the table. I give him a grin and take a bite. "It's decent, I promise. Just try it."

"Adam, is something wrong?" Steve voice is soft and placating. He's handling me with kid gloves again.

More distractions in his already chaotic life. He doesn't need to worry about me anymore. I'm great. I know what I'm doing. I've got a plan.

"Not at all, Ace." I wink at the use of Joey's nickname for him. "I'm fine. Just focus on taking care of Joey and don't worry about me at all."

I shovel another forkful into my mouth. "Eat, eat. It's good."

Steve finally takes a bite and nods appreciatively. "It is good, sweetie. Thank you for cooking."

~**~

On Friday night, I'm putting my toiletries in my duffle bag when Steve walks in. "Hey, sweetheart. What are you up to?"

"Just finished packing for this weekend." I point to my boots. "Will those shoes be okay or should I run out to Macy's to buy a waterproof pair?"

"This weekend?" Steve's lips fall into a frown. "Shit, sweetheart. I'm so sorry. I thought I told you about Kurt's funeral. It's tomorrow afternoon and Joey really wants to go. We'll have to reschedule to another time."

"Oh." I sit on my bed with my hands folded in my lap. "Yeah, that's fine."

Steve sits next to me and pulls me onto his lap. "I'm sorry, babe. I know this is disappointing. I'm disappointed too. But Joey needs this closure. He's having a hard time accepting that he did everything he could to save Kurt." Steve shakes his head then presses his lips to my temple. I keep my eyes locked on the bedside lamp. It feels good to be in Steve's arms. Held by his strong body. Protected. I focus my whole body on just feeling Steve around me. This is what I'll be thinking about. This moment is what will give me the courage to do what I need to do.

"But I promise we'll go soon. Next weekend if the bungalow is available. If not, the first available weekend after that."

I nod because that's what he's waiting for. Actually, he's waiting for words but he doesn't push when I remain mute.

Steve's body rocks back and forth, lulling me like a baby. I almost wish I could stay in his arms forever. Never have to leave him or Joey. But I know that's not possible. Not anymore. And as if to punctuate that thought, Joey let's out a wail that makes me shiver in sympathy pain.

Steve stands quickly and places me on my feet. As soon as I'm steady, he is up the stairs, tending to his lover. The only one that holds his heart. The only one who will ever hold his heart.

CHAPTER TWENTY

STEVE

Funerals suck. I avoid them like the plague, but Joey needed me today so I held his hand, and sometimes his whole body, and we made it through the service.

As we're driving home, I think about how Adam has been acting. His entire demeanor changed overnight. One minute he's normal and the next he's, Stepford. For the past twenty-four hours, he's been practically skipping through the house, as if life is wonderful.

Granted, life is pretty wonderful in general, but I know he's not callous enough to find joy in Joey's pain. That's not it, but there is definitely something going on in that pretty little head of his.

As the sky opens up and water pelts down on my truck, a pit begins to form in my stomach. A strange foreboding overwhelms me and I hit the accelerator a little faster.

"You okay, Ace?" Joey's hand lands on my knee.

I shake my head, thinking of a faster route home. Something is wrong. Definitely wrong.

"I'm worried about Adam." I wanted him to come with us. Almost begged. But he insisted on staying home. He said he had stuff to take care of. I should have asked what stuff he meant. But the look in his eyes when we left was so...vacant.

Fuck! Why didn't I recognize it sooner?

"Adam?" Joey reaches for his phone and is already dialing before I can respond. "Why? What's wrong with Adam?"

I reach for Joey's hand and hold it against my chest as I race home. "I hope nothing, but he's been acting strange. Like happy. But not in a regular happy kind of way. Like he's found peace."

Joey knows what I mean. He's seen enough troubled youth to know that people don't just find peace one day. For most people, that doesn't come until they make the decision to go after that elusive peace. The kind of peace that only comes with death.

"He's not answering his phone." Joey's voice is frantic and I hate worrying him. Everything is probably fine and I'm creating stress where there shouldn't be any. But I can't shake the feeling that Adam is in trouble. Desperate trouble.

"Call the house."

We're just blocks away but it seems like miles. Continents away from saving the one person that Joey and I have grown to need in our lives. In our family.

"It's going to voicemail."

I hang the corner a little too fast and the rear end fishtails, but we don't spin out. Thankfully. A car accident is the last thing I need to deal with at this second.

"911. Get an ambulance."

Joey is now in tears, forcing steady words into the phone when we finally get to the house. I don't bother with the garage. I park the car in the driveway and jump out, rushing the door like my life depends on it. In some way, it does.

If anything happens to Adam, neither Joey nor I will ever be the same. In just the few short months he's been with us, he's changed the whole dynamic of our family. As if we were just waiting for him to arrive, everything came together once he was here.

We need him.

The front door is unlocked so I barrel through and run into Adam's room. The shower is running and I let out a relieved sigh. He's just taking a shower. That's why he didn't answer the phone.

I'm about to tell Joey to cancel the ambulance when I realize water is coming from beneath the bathroom door.

"Adam!" I growl out his name but don't wait for a response. My shoulder pushes through the door with a quiet snap and my stomach drops to my feet. Adam is lying in an overflowing tub. The pink water only confirms what I suspected on my way home. In the distance I hear sounds that I pray are sirens. The sirens we need to save Adam.

His head is hanging back against the wall but he's completely unresponsive. I turn off the freezing water and pull Adam's limp body from the tub in one broad sweep. His chest isn't moving up or down but I refuse to believe we've lost him. We can't be too late. Carrying Adam to the bed, my hot tears fall onto his pale skin.

Please let him be okay.

"No, no, no." Joey crumbles to the ground as the sirens become louder. "Steve, please don't let him die."

I fold the comforter over Adam's cold skin and hold him until the paramedics arrive, only pulling myself off his body when they are ready to tend to him.

"Joey, call Dylan."

Joey picks up his phone in a zombie-like state as the paramedics begin to ask me questions. I don't know the answers they're looking for but I tell them what I can while watching Adam get loaded onto a rolling stretcher.

"I'm going with him." I follow the stretcher, lifting Joey off the ground as we head to the front door. "Is Dylan coming?"

Joey nods, probably going into shock himself.

"Joey, baby." His eyes dart around for a moment before he focuses on me. "You need to wait here for

Dylan. He'll bring you to the hospital. But I have to go now, okay?"

Joey nods, more tears flowing. At least I know he's present and aware. "Okay. I'll wait for Dylan."

I pull a throw blanket off the sofa and wrap up Joey like a burrito. "I love you, baby. I'll see you in a few minutes."

"Take care of him, Ace. Make sure he comes back to us," Joey whispers as I shut the door behind me.

~**~

A failed suicide attempt. That's what they call it. I call it a fucking miracle. The only word in there that matters is failed.

Adam's going to survive.

Joey and I have been taking turns at his bedside for the past twelve hours. He's still sedated from the surgery he needed to close up the cut across his radial artery but it wasn't lethal. It clotted faster than it could bleed out. Thank fuck!

The doctor thinks Adam passed out from shock of the injury and from the cold water. He was in the beginning stage of hypothermia when we found him.

God, that was the scariest moment of my life. I've been in some bad situations in my time but seeing someone I love on the brink of death is not something I'll ever forget.

My hands are wrapped around Adam's bicep. I just need to feel his warm, pink skin so I can get the image of his pale and lifeless body out of my head forever.

I rest my forehead on Adam's arm and close my eyes. He should wake up soon. The doctor said he'd wake up at any time and that was forty minutes ago. "Please, babe. Wake up for me. I need to see those gorgeous teal eyes of yours."

He doesn't even twitch. "I'm so sorry we let you down, Adam. We were so caught up in our own shit that we didn't see what was happening with you. I don't know what triggered this but I will do everything in my power to make sure you never feel hopeless again, babe. Joey and I love you. We need you, sweetheart. Please wake up."

A sob breaks through from my chest and I squeeze his arm. "Dammit, Adam. Wake the fuck up and look at me."

The sound of a gasping breath steals my own as I look at Adam's face. His eyes are still closed but his lips pull apart as he inhales deeply, as if he's been underwater for a few seconds too long.

"Adam." I use my commanding voice. The low tone that always gets an instant response from him. "Open your eyes."

Adam's left cheek twitches and his eyes screw shut. An overhead light is pointed right at his face so I push it away, allowing a shadow to fall across his beautiful face.

"Now, Adam. Open your eyes."

Adam's eyelids slowly pull apart. It takes a minute for his eyes to adjust but when they do, they don't stray from mine. "Steve?"

His voice is raspy, no louder than a whisper, but it's the sweetest sound I've ever heard.

"I'm right here, babe." I stand over him so he can see me without having to move his head. "I'll always be right here."

Chapter Twenty-One

Joey

HE'S AWAKE.

When I see the text from Steve, it takes my addled brain a minute to understand it. I stand up from the table in the cafeteria I'm sitting at with Dylan and Spencer.

"He's awake. Steve says he's awake."

The cafeteria is on the first floor and Adam is on the fifth floor. I pound the elevator button, hoping that'll make the fucking doors open faster.

Dylan's large fist closes over mine and holds it above the button. "It's coming, kid. Just wait two seconds."

As if on cue, the doors open and an elderly woman is pushing an even more elderly man in a wheelchair. I'm ready to shove them out of the damn lift when Spencer steps in.

"Let me help you, ma'am." He pushes the man out of the elevator then offers his arm to the woman. "Where are you heading?"

"Our van will pick us up in parking lot B."

Spencer tosses an amused smile over his shoulder and mouths, "I'll meet you up there."

I manage to get in four good smacks of the number five button before Dylan tugs me away from the panel.

"What did that button ever do to you?" he says, pulling me into his arms. "We're almost there. Just take deep breaths."

"He's awake, Dyl. He's okay."

Dylan rubs a hand down my back. "I know, kid. It's okay now. Everything is going to be okay."

The doors open and I pull away from Dylan and run down the hall, slowing only when I pass the nurses' station. I barrel into Adam's room and see the most beautiful sight.

Steve is kissing Adam fully on the mouth. It's so tender. So gentle. And so fucking hot. I move to the other side of the bed so I can say hello too.

Steve ends the kiss then cups the back of my head and pulls me in for a quick peck. His eyes are red-rimmed and puffy. I know he's been crying but these must be tears of joy. I know mine are.

I look down at Adam and watch one of my tears land on his cheek, mixing with one of his. "Hey, honey. I'm happy to see you're awake."

Adam nods and more tears fall. "I'm so sorry, guys. I didn't want to hurt you anymore. I felt responsible for Kurt's death and—"

"What?" Steve and I both say it at the same time.

I shake my head, trying to understand what he's talking about. "How could you possibly be responsible for Kurt's death? You didn't even know him."

"But you stopped looking for him. You said it was your fault he wasn't saved...and it was my fault you stopped looking."

"No, honey." I hold his cheeks in my palms and stare right into his eyes. "It wasn't my fault and it sure as hell wasn't your fault. Honestly, it was Kurt's fault. He shot up. He'd been doing it most of his life and he didn't want to stop. I think he knew this was how things would end for him. I'm sorry we couldn't save him but I don't blame myself or you."

Adam eyes are downcast, even though I'm holding his face toward me. "Well, I'm sorry for what I did. I thought I was causing you too much trouble and you'd be better off without me."

"We're not." Steve's booming voice reverberates off the stainless steel in the room. "We're better with you, Adam. Don't you see that?"

He shrugs. "I want that to be true. I want it so badly. I just..."

"Words, sweetheart. Say what you're thinking."

"I'm just worried that I'm falling in love with you guys, but I'll always just be a toy for you. A human toy, but a toy nonetheless. Something you can find amusement in when you want to, but never a real part of your relationship."

"That's how you feel?" I ask, heartbroken that we haven't done a better job of showing Adam his value in our life. His importance to our family even after just a few months.

"That's what I think."

Steve growls then whispers into Adam's ear, "Well, we'll just have to change that pretty little mind of yours."

~**~

We have to wait until the evening shift change before Adam is released. Because he doesn't have insurance, the hospital was all too eager to discharge him so he didn't take up a bed overnight.

Steve arranged to pay for his medical bills, but they still like to move people out as quickly as possible unless a fat HMO is footing the bill.

Adam is weak but can walk into the house alone. Instead of asking where he wants to sleep, Steve guides Adam to the staircase.

"It's okay, Steve." Adam sounds embarrassed, despite his soft voice. "You don't have to babysit me. I promise not to do anything stupid."

"I'm not babysitting you, and I'm not taking no for an answer." Steve wraps an arm around Adam's waist and almost carries him up the stairs. "You're sleeping with us from now on."

I have to bite down on my cheek to stop the ear-to-ear grin.

"You don't have—"

"This isn't open for discussion, Adam."

Adam's whole body seems to melt into Steve as they climb the last few stairs to the top. When we get to our bedroom, Steve and I carefully undress Adam.

He's eyes are only half open, but he holds up his arms and steps out of his pants when we ask him to. As soon as he's fully nude, I pull back the comforter and Adam slips between the sheets.

I start to undress but Steve turns toward the door. "I'm gonna grab a few waters. Do you need anything else, baby?"

"No, thanks." I slide my jeans off my hips and let them pool at my feet. Steve's eyes glow as he takes in my body. "But hurry back. We need you."

Steve nods curtly then jogs downstairs. He's naked and on the other side of Adam within ninety seconds.

Adam curls into Steve's chest and I press against his back. If the heat radiating off our bodies is too much, Adam doesn't complain. He locks us all together with bent elbows and hooked ankles, ensuring the three of us stay connected throughout the night.

I enjoy waking up to a lazy hand job, most guys probably do, but opening my eyes to Adam stroking me while he swallows Steve's enormous cock is beyond hot. I don't even get time to fully enjoy it before I'm shooting my load onto my thighs and belly.

Steve twists at his waist and places a wet kiss on my mouth. "Good morning, little duck."

"Uh yeah." I rub the cooling puddle off my belly and wipe my hand on the sheet. It'll need to be washed anyway. "Definitely a good morning."

I sit up fully and hover over Steve so I can kiss him properly. Tugging at the ring in his left nipple causes him to moan in my mouth. I reach for his right nipple as he bucks up into Adam's face, burying his cock as far as it can go.

Adam's face turns red but he doesn't pull away. In fact, from where I'm sitting, it looks like he's pressing even harder into Steve, trying to get deeper.

"God, Adam." Steve's hand fists Adam's hair before his fingers relax and stroke his head. "Your mouth is so hot."

CHAPTER TWENTY-TWO

STEVE

As insecure as Adam can be sometimes, he definitely knows how to suck dick. I'm thick and slightly above average in the length department so most guys can't get my head past their throat. But Adam works me in like butter. Smooth and silky heat surrounds me, substituting well for his ass, which is currently off limits.

He's made it clear that he doesn't fuck. Joey has tried to get his reasons from him but he's not ready to talk. And that's okay. We won't push him to give more than he's ready for.

If and when he wants to take that step, Joey and I will be here for him. Waiting. Ready. Until then, his mouth will do just fine.

Adam sucks every last drop out of me, keeping my head in his mouth like a lollypop even while looking up at me and Joey shyly.

"If I had known this is how you like to wake up, I would have insisted you sleep with us weeks ago." I wink at Adam and am rewarded with a beaming grin.

"That looks like fun," Joey says, repositioning himself so he's kneeling over Adam. "Can I try that on you?"

Adam exhales through his nose and nods, presenting his perfectly curved cock to Joey. "Mmm, it looks yummy, but I'll need to taste it to be sure."

Joey kisses Adam's knee then leaves a slick tongue trail all the way up to his balls. Adam releases my tip from his lips and throws his head back against the mattress, fully enjoying Joey's touch.

The erotic scene in front of me is beyond words. Both men are so beautiful. So full of love. So…mine.

With my cock lengthening again, I slip out of the bed and grab the lube from my nightstand.

I grease up my cock and stand behind the bed, stroking myself back up to full mast.

Joey has a slow but steady rhythm on Adam's cock, pulling off then sucking in again. My little duck doesn't break his stride at all when my hands close on his hips and I press my shaft against his ass. He merely pushes back and tilts his pelvis up and down so my dick is sliding along his crease.

I push my middle finger past Joey's tight muscle and see his body break out in goose pimples. My boy loves when I'm inside him. After pumping in and out a few times, I slide in a second finger, scissoring them apart to fully relax his opening.

Joey has amazing control over his body and knows how to fully open for me. With just a minute or two of prep, his ass is humping my hand and his mouth whimpers for more.

The sounds and vibrations must catch Adam's attention because he finally opens his eyes and sees what I'm doing. We haven't had any penetration around Adam because he's still uncomfortable with the idea. But if he's going to be fully in this relationship, he's going to see what we really do. The good, the bad, and the fucking hot as hell.

This moment falls into that last category. Pushing my dick into Joey's eager ass while he sucks off Adam is more sensual than anything I've ever done. No toys or groups or scenes in clubs could hold a candle to this moment with Joey and Adam.

Creating a chain of passion and trust with the men I love.

Even though I just came a few minutes ago, I can feel my balls drawing up as I thrust in and out of Joey's tight channel.

His hand has moved to his cock but I chase it down and push it away. "Let me help you with that, baby."

"Fuck, Ace." Joey's tongue traces the underside of Adam's cock while his fingers tease his balls. "This feels so good. All of it."

Adam's hand clamps around the base of his cock. "God, I'm close, guys."

Joey immediately closes his lips over Adam's head and sucks hard. His hollowed cheeks and Adam's full balls provide all the visual stimulation I need to crash over the edge.

Pumping two more times into Joey's ass, I shoot into him, filling his tight hole with my seed.

I stroke Joey even faster, hearing the familiar change in his breathing. He's there. Joey comes in my hand, moaning with Adam's dick still nestled down his throat.

Adam cries out as I ride the pulsing contractions around my drowning cock. This moment will be etched in my mind forever.

We take our time getting out of bed and showering. This is the first day of our life together. Our family feels complete and we can move forward knowing we each play a role in the happiness of the other two men we share our bed with.

Chapter Twenty-Three

Adam (Two Months Later)

Whatever I hoped to accomplish with my little stunt in the bathtub is not what happened. I don't know what I expected but I think it was my way of telling Steve and Joey that I knew they didn't need me.

What I accomplished instead is learning how fully and completely they want me. They use the word love and I believe that's what I feel for the two amazing men in my life. But I know that will evolve over time.

In just the past few weeks since I moved into their bedroom, and more completely into their lives, our connection has evolved every day. It grows stronger, deeper, hotter as we discover new things about each other and how we fit together.

Steve's thirtieth birthday is today, even though the party Joey planned with all of their friends isn't until Saturday. But Joey and I want to do something special for Steve tonight. Just the three of us—the family.

Rachel is closing up the kiosk for me tonight so I've been cooking all afternoon. Knowing Steve is a meat and potatoes man, I've prepared beef Wellington and new potatoes with black truffles.

I've prepared this dish at school but never had a chance to cook it for someone that might appreciate it. I'm nervous about how it will taste, but I know Steve will be gracious regardless. And for dessert, I have peach pies in the oven. Steve's favorite. At least, that's dessert number one. I have another surprise planned for later, but that's after we get through the meal.

"We're home." Joey opens the door and closes his eyes, inhaling deeply. "Oh, honey. It smells so good in here."

"Mmm, it does. What's the occasion?" Steve asks innocently as he trails behind Joey.

"No occasion." I tease, leaning forward so Joey can kiss my mouth. Steve's lips follow right behind Joey's. "Just felt like cooking."

"Well, I hope this non-occasion food is ready soon because I'm starving." Steve pats my ass then heads to the fridge. "Beer?"

"Yes, please." I pull the beef out of the oven and set it on the counter to rest.

"Me too." Joey pulls plates from the cabinet and disappears into the dining room.

Steve and Joey are always generous with their compliments, but they are over-the-top gushing over dinner. It's just a steak in puff pastry, but they're happy, so I'm happy.

After we each enjoy a slice of pie, Joey and I put the second half of our surprise in motion.

"Why don't you wait for us upstairs, Ace?" Joey suggests.

"Upstairs?" His sexy grin and darkening eyes tells us he knows we're up to something.

"Yeah, um." I step into his chest and place my hand over his heart. "Just get comfortable on the bed and we'll be up in a minute."

"Like," Steve waggles his eyebrows in a silly gesture, "naked comfortable?"

"Just go before we change our minds." Joey shoves Steve's massive body toward the staircase. "Close the door and don't open it. We'll let ourselves in when we're ready."

"I'll be anxiously awaiting your arrival." Steve disappears up the stairs.

As soon as we hear the door shut behind him, Joey turns to me. "Okay, so you have the music ready?"

I nod. "It's downloaded and ready. We just have to tell Alexa to play the song." The Echo Steve put in the bedroom has been one of the coolest gadgets I've ever played with. We've spent hours in bed trying to outdo each other by selecting sexy songs to mess around to.

"So we're ready?" Joey asks.

"I'm ready. Do you think Steve's settled in yet?"

"That man can shed his clothes in two point four seconds if he thinks something kinky is coming." Joey laughs. "Trust me, he's ready."

"Let's do it."

Joey takes my hand and leads me up the stairs. We strip down to our boxer briefs before opening the door. Slipping a hand against the wall, I turn off the overhead light. "Alexa, turn on the lamp."

The lamp on Steve's tall dresser blinks on and the room is cast in a warm glow. Joey pushes the door completely open so Steve can see us draped against each other in the dim light.

"Holy fuck!" Steve says under his breath.

"Alexa, play *Take Me to Church*."

We wait for the first few chords to play before Joey and I slink into the room, slowly walking to the beat of the slow, sensual song. I turn right and Joey turns left, putting on a show for our man.

I can't decide if I should be watching Joey's smooth, graceful movements or the hungry way Steve's gaze moves from left to right, keeping us both in his field of vision.

Easing our man of his dilemma, Joey and I meet up at the foot of the bed so he can easily see us. Joey reaches for my chin and turns me to face him. His tongue drags along my jaw until he reaches my mouth. Pulling my lower lip between his teeth, Joey moans out loud.

My arm wraps around Joey and I lean against his chest, attacking his mouth. He tastes so good. Our cocks are both hard and pressed together beneath the thin layers of fabric separating them.

"My god, you're so beautiful." Steve's gravelly voice makes me smile against Joey's lips. Joey grinds harder and shifts a few degrees so more of my back is on display to Steve's smoldering gaze.

Joey's fingertips dance down my spine then dip below the waistband of my boxers. He hooks a finger under the elastic and tugs slightly. Only half a cheek is exposed, but the slow reveal earns us a frustrated groan from Steve.

I press back, wiggling my ass for Steve's benefit. Joey's other hand slides under my shorts and pulls the other side down. With the fabric positioned halfway down my ass, Joey spins me around, stepping directly behind me.

My cock is sticking straight up, preventing my underwear from sliding down my legs. With my back resting on his chest, Joey's hands roam my heated flesh.

Fingers glide across my nipples.

Teeth nip at my earlobe.

Sweat beads on my forehead.

Fuck, I need more.

Joey ravishes my neck, making wet, slopping sounds as his hands free my seeping cock from its cotton barrier. My boxers drop to the floor and Joey's hands get to work. One palm flattens on my belly and slides down, evading my dick to stop gently on my balls. Joey cups my sack while his other hand closes around my shaft.

Joey's dick is nestled in my crack. He rocks up and down while his hand strokes me in a slow and gentle rhythm.

As the song comes to an end, Joey's hand slips around my hip and lands on the small of my back. He presses with just enough force that I lean forward onto the bed.

Climbing on all fours, I wait for Joey to join me then we crawl up the bed, stalking our prey from both sides.

Steve has pulled the sheet off his lap and is stroking his engorged cock, tugging the tip as he watches us without blinking.

"Happy birthday, Steve," I say, dropping a wet kiss on Steve's thigh, swirling my tongue through the hair before biting gently.

"We love you, Ace." Joey kisses Steve's other thigh.

We nip and lick our way to his center. Steve's hand leaves his lap as he gives us space to play.

Joey pulls Steve's knee up and back then climbs over it so he has full access to Steve's balls. I curl my head over Steve's stomach and nuzzle the soft curls before darting my tongue out and tasting his glistening tip.

Finally, I suck him into my mouth, relishing the sweet tang that meets my tongue. He tastes so good. So manly.

I inhale his shaft down my throat then swallow around his wide head. God, he's amazing.

Joey rolls Steve's hip forward then digs into his ass, eating it out with sloshy moans.

I work Steve's dick in and out a few more times before pulling off and kissing his mouth. Steve holds me to him like his life depends on it. "That was so fucking hot, sweetheart."

I smile and nip at his jaw. "Steve?"

His palm curls around my cheek, his thumb brushing over my tender lips. "Yes, Adam."

"Will you fuck me?"

The room is silent as both Joey and Steve stop breathing. Joey's hand rests on my thigh, offering me the comfort I can always count on from him.

"Adam, love." Steve's eyes are unwavering even though his voice cracks. "Are you sure that's what you want?"

I nod and kiss Steve's earlobe then reach for Joey's hand. "I really do. I trust you—both of you—not to hurt me."

Steve turns to catch my lip in his teeth, tugging me gently before running his tongue along it. "We'll never hurt you. I promise. We love you, sweetheart. You've made this an amazing birthday for me."

He pauses briefly, looking to Joey and then back to me.

"You've made this an amazing...life...for me. You and Joey have quickly become...well, everything for me."

Steve sits up and pulls me onto his lap, just holding me in his strong arms. Completely lost in the heat of his lips on mine, massaging and caressing me, I don't even realize he's moved me onto my back until Joey's bicep slides under my neck and he curls into my side.

Steve's lips are replaced by Joey's as Steve licks a path from my neck down to my balls. Warm saliva drips into my crease and my spine tenses.

Joey's hand moves to my dick as Steve's tongue kisses my hole with the same loving tenderness he used on my mouth just moments ago.

I've never enjoyed penetration. It's never been an act I could associate with pleasure or intimacy. After leaving Paddles, and swearing I'd never let another man use me for sex again, I gave up the idea. I enjoyed oral and physical stimulation. That was enough.

But after watching Steve take Joey so gently, so sensually, I've wanted to give myself to him. To both of them. I know they'll take care of me in a way I've never been cared for before.

Steve's tongue prods my hole as I exhale slowly against Joey's cheek, reminding myself that it's Steve. Not Lee. Not a trick. And not the bastard that raped me when I was only fourteen.

Steve loves me and won't ever hurt me.

His tongue breaks through my pucker and my breath hitches. Not from fear or pain, but from relief. And lust.

Fuck, it feels good.

A finger prods my opening, stiffer than the tongue but still gentle. Steve is taking his time, opening me up so I can take his girth with as little pain as possible.

Joey's hot breath is at my ear, distracting me from the intrusion below. "You're so brave, honey. You're giving Steve a gift he would have never asked for."

"It's for you too." I pant the words, barely able to speak through the mixed sensations flooding every nerve ending.

"I love you, Adam." Joey's teeth close on my shoulder, gently sucking just as Steve's fingers move out of me. "I'd be honored to share that with you some day."

Steve is back with the blunt tip of his head nudging at my hole. "Are you sure you're ready for me, sweetheart?"

"Yes." I reach for my dick and stroke it, slowly bringing it back to attention. "Take me. Please."

Joey's head drops to my crotch and he sucks in my head at the same moment Steve slides past my rim.

"Oh god." My fists ball up the sheets and my jaw clenches as I breathe through the intrusion. It's been a long time since I've had anything inside me, and no one has ever been as wide as Steve is.

White hot pain shoots through my body, but it doesn't last long. Within seconds, the pain of Steve's thick cock is overshadowed by the silky suction of Joey's tongue.

I don't know when it happens, but I find myself bucking into Joey's mouth and dropping down to meet Steve's thrusts with equal enthusiasm.

My fist unwraps from the sheet as the tension in my body evaporates. My fingernails rake across Joey's short hair, tugging him up and down as he sucks my dick to the same rhythm Steve has going in my ass.

I'm genuinely surprised when the first trace of an orgasm fills my gut. I didn't expect to get off with Steve in me. It would be a first, but then again, Steve and Joey are responsible for many of my firsts.

I thrust harder into Joey's mouth and pound deeper onto Steve's cock.

Holy fuck!

Steve's angle changes as he leans over Joey's back. My mind and body explode at the same time. Waves of pleasure rock through me as I spill into Joey's mouth, filling him with the same juices I hope Steve will fill me with.

We had the STD discussion weeks ago, but I never thought I'd put that knowledge to practical use. Now, I'm grateful Steve is completely bare as his feral growls echo in the sex-fogged room. He pushes deeper into me than I would have thought possible while he fills me with wet heat.

My eyes lock with Steve's as he pulses inside me, filling me with his seed the way I just did to Joey.

Joey kisses the tip of my cock then moves so he's snuggled against my side. Steve lowers his head and licks up the streaks of pearly white come painted across Joey's belly.

I didn't even notice Joey's release, so caught up in my own. I'll need to get better at monitoring and meeting the needs of my lovers. I want them to feel the same love and devotion they've shown me since the first night I arrived.

We truly do complete each other in a strange yet natural way. I wouldn't give this up for anything in the world, and I'm finally starting to realize that I'll never have to.

Meet Alex in Denver in
Mile High Romance #1: When It's Right

When Shane Greenly left his home in Casper Mountain, WY, he was leaving more than just the closet. He needed a fresh start to pursue his dream of running a dog training ranch without having to deny who he really is.

Meeting Alex was one of the best things that could have happened to Shane. They were at the beginning of a wonderful relationship when the unthinkable happened and Shane had to leave. The consequences of his past mistakes could not be hidden any longer.

More M/M Romance books by Aria Grace:

More Than Friends series

More Than Friends (#1)*

Drunk in Love (#2)*

Choosing Happy (#3)*

Just Stay (#4)*

Hands On (#5)*

Best Chance (#6)*

My Name is Luka (#7)*

Finally Found (#8)*

Looking For Home (#9)*

Choosing Us (#10)*

Mile High Romance series

When It's Right (#1)*

When I'm Weak (#2)*

When I'm Lost (#3)*

When You Were Mine (#4)*

When I Fall (#5)*

When Whiskey Stops Working (#6)

Promises Series
(M/M and M/F Contemporary)

Break Me Like a Promise (#1)

Trust Me Like a Promise (#2)

Keep Me Like a Promise (#3)

Real Answers Investigations series

Corner Office (#1)*

Soy Latte (#2)*

Cheers To That (#3)

Standalones

His Undoing (Gay For You)*

Winter Chill (First Time Gay)*

Escaping in Oz (College First Time)

*Also available as an audiobook

If you enjoyed this book, please consider leaving a review. Indie authors need all the support we can get. Thanks so much!

Learn more at www.AriaGraceBooks.com or become a kick ass fan and join my mailing list for updates and free book opportunities.

ariagracebooks@gmail.com

https://twitter.com/AriaGraceBooks

https://www.facebook.com/ariagracebooks

http://youtube.com/ariagracebooks

http://www.amazon.com/author/ariagrace

56457034R00120

Made in the USA
Lexington, KY
22 October 2016